THE BARRIER

The Barrier
by
Carmen Anthony Fiore

Townhouse Publishing
Princeton, New Jersey 08540

Original hardcover edition published July 1964 by
Pageant Press, Inc. of New York.

First trade paperback edition published December 1986 by
Townhouse Publishing, 301 N. Harrison Street, Bldg.-B,
Suite 115, Princeton, NJ 08540

Manufactured in the United States of America

ISBN 0-939219-01-8 (PBK)

to my wife
CATHERINE

"The young leading the young
is like the blind leading the blind."

Lord Chesterfield
Letter to his son,
November 6, 1747.

CHAPTER 1

Bobbie Lee was illegitimate. He was derived from a secret union between two Negro field hands in a tenant shack on an Alabama peanut farm. During that chilly November evening inside the cluttered, stuffy bedroom, Lottie Mae and her lover butted against each other without a feeling of love—just pure animal passion. And after excited movements and moans of sexual pleasure, Bobbie Lee was conceived in Lottie Mae Lee's hot, quivering body.

Nine months later, she gave birth to a full-term six-pound, healthy baby boy, hardly a month before moving north.

Lottie Mae had decided to accompany her aunt and uncle on their trip to New Sussex. Despite her youth, she sensed a barren future working on the farm and hoped for a better life in the North.

They abandoned the farmer's life on a clear, mild, September day. The four hopeful travelers included Lottie Mae, her middle-aged, gregarious Uncle, Curtis Lee, her rotund, subdued, but friendly Aunt Murrel and Lottie Mae's month-old baby, Bobbie.

At nineteen, Lottie Mae was attractive. She had black curly hair that had a slight kink to it and her face was small, oval-shaped with a narrow, delicate nose and lips in a continual pout. Her skin was honey-brown, smooth and softly textured, like finely woven silk.

Pensive and uneasy, Lottie Mae sat in the bumpy rear

seat and nibbled on her lower lip. She always bit her lip when she felt anxious. Lottie Mae held Bobbie closely during most of the long, wearisome trip northward.

When their dilapidated Ford sedan, 1932 vintage, finally labored into Mercerton, New Sussex hampered by a bearing knock and a boiling radiator, the hopeful group of wartime pioneers headed immediately to the over-crowded Negro ghetto—South Mercerton.

It was a typical Negro community during World War II, filling rapidly with emigrants from the South attracted by bustling factories and high wages. The red brick, row houses were bursting with people. Six-room houses became five, one-room efficiency apartments sharing a common bathroom and kitchen.

Lottie Mae and Bobbie shared a one-room apartment with Uncle Curtis and Aunt Murrel. This arrangement permitted Lottie Mae to work, while Aunt Murrel watched Bobbie; factory work during the war, housework after the war.

Washing and cleaning was hard work for Lottie Mae's small, thin frame. Her arms tired easily and her back hurt. She wondered why she left the farm; housecleaning was just as hard. She was becoming unhappy with her new life in the North.

Lottie Mae made only one close friend during the first year in Mercerton. She was quiet and seldom volunteered friendship. It took a forceful person to get Lottie Mae out of her shell. And Bernice Alliston was just that type. She was definitely outgoing and aggressive, tempered by an urge to be friendly—a strong herd instinct.

Bernice Alliston was burly, like a big female gorilla. Her skin was black and coarse. She had a wide friendly face with large white teeth that stuck out of her mouth when she laughed or smiled. With her deep, husky voice, she could rattle glasses in a closet.

2

Bernice was sitting on the only chair in the room. It was near the closed window; shut to keep out the dampness. The chair was hardly strong enough to support her. She overlapped it considerably.

Lottie Mae looked even tinier on the long sofa. Her oval face was drawn with fatigue. Dark circles hung beneath her eyes in contrast with her light brown skin. She was biting her lower lip and breathing through her mouth, making an occasional sucking sound. The congestion in her lungs and sinuses made her feel miserable. The damp, cold weather added to her miseries.

Bernice felt sorry for Lottie Mae, and hated to see her so pitiful. She decided to speak her mind. "Lottie Mae. I knows ya hates doin' days work. Killin' yo'self, cleanin' people's houses." She paused, wiped her mouth with her right hand and continued; "Tol' ya las' month. Ya oughta get on relief. Knows ya can."

"Never paid it no mind," answered Lottie Mae. Her lower lip swollen and stinging where the skin was bitten away. She examined her lip and winced when she pressed too hard.

"Look at me, honey. Where do ya thinks I gets my nice clothes . . . feeds my kids? Breakin' my back, scrubbin' dirty flo's?" Bernice asked and unfolded her arms to offer a full view of her new dress.

"Ya do has nice clothes," Lottie Mae replied, a hint of yearning in her soft voice as she looked at her faded blue housedress. It was shabby and she suddenly felt ashamed in front of her well-dressed friend.

"I'as been on relief, since las' year. Ain't had it so good," confessed the ex-field hand. "Ain't never gonna catch me doin' no mo' hard work, no how!" Bernice bellowed, while spraying the air with saliva.

"Is ya sho I can get on, without no trouble?"

"Ain't got no husband t' suppo't ya," Bernice replied.

"If the daddy ain't around here. Can't be got no place else. You an' the kid gets on." She sprayed saliva towards Lottie Mae.

"Ain't 'round here no place," Lottie Mae indicated with a sweep of her arm. "Gonna be hard t' find down Alabama."

Bernice leaned forward and patted Lottie Mae's thin arm. The arm's smooth skin, contrasting with the heavy, rough hand. "Don't worry none. Won't be nasty t' ya." Bernice gave Lottie Mae's arm a friendly squeeze, smiled and whispered, "Ev'rythin' gonna be jus' fine."

The red lines in Lottie Mae's eyes betrayed her anxious feelings. She began nibbling at her lip but had to stop. It still hurt. "What's I gonna tell 'em 'bout the daddy?" Her voice, breathless and quivering; "Don't know his las' name!"

"Don't worry none. Jus' tell 'em the truth." Bernice stood up, reached for her coat and said, "Be ready by nine. Gonna take ya down t'morra, myself." She wiped her mouth with her right hand, said good-bye and treaded heavily out of the room.

The next morning, Bernice led the hesitant Lottie Mae to the welfare office. They were the first to arrive, and were ushered into the reception office. It was a small, drab, stuffy room with a cluttered desk. They had to wait about fifteen minutes, before the caseworker arrived.

Lottie Mae looked up and saw an unfriendly face in the doorway. The face was annoyed. Its lips pursed tightly, eyes edged by crow's feet. It was surrounded by a half-combed mass of graying black hair.

"Good morning. I'm Mrs. Neves."

Lottie Mae and Bernice mumbled greetings and waited.

Alma Neves cleared the clutter away put three appli-

4

cation forms and two carbons into the typewriter and began the inquiry: Lottie Mae's name, age, address and next of kin with a repeat for Bobbie.

After the routine questions were over, the important question still needed to be answered. Alma Neves stared directly into Lottie Mae's black eyes and asked "What is the status of the father?"

"The what?" Lottie Mae asked. A bewildered expression covered her face. She looked for help from Bernice, who shrugged her shoulders and pleaded ignorance.

Impatient tapping of the pen; "His whereabouts. His name. His address. Is he supporting the child?" Alma Neves stopped and waited for the answers. She made a ninety degree turn in the swivel chair and faced Lottie Mae with strained patience.

"Oh . . . ain't seen him, since I came no'th. Name is Jesse." She paused. "Never did tell me his las' name." After a second pause, she continued; "Never did find out where he went." Lottie Mae sucked in her lower lip, hesitated, then confessed; "Ain't never seen Bobbie. . . . Don't know he's the daddy!" After she said it, she stopped, her black eyes floated in tears, blurring her vision. She started biting her lower lip again.

Alma Neves watched Lottie Mae's shaking, nervous signature on the original and the two carbon copies, folded the second carbon copy and gave it to Lottie Mae. "This is your copy. A caseworker will visit you to complete the investigation. She'll inspect your home situation and verify your child's birth certificate and shot records." Alma Neves stepped quickly to the door, opened it and ended the interview; "Thank you and good day."

Lottie Mae soon lost interest in domestic work, and depended entirely on the welfare's monthly check.

She moved out of the crowded apartment, acquiring

more livable quarters: a cozy, three-room apartment on the third floor in a neighborhood that was changing from white to colored.

Within a month she had a male companion to help pass her leisure hours and help celebrate on check day which was the first of every month. This was the highest standard of living Lottie Mae ever knew; a long country mile from the shack and peanut fields in Alabama. She was really living! The relaxed life put a few extra pounds on her thin, delicate frame and hips. Her face even filled out. The hollow, almost sunken cheeks looked fuller, greatly improving her features. Her man thought she was becoming "real nice!"

Lottie Mae's man was Joe Wilson, who stood six feet in shoes and had powerfully built arms and chest—the result of strenuous laboring jobs. He loved to work in the hot sun; sweating and singing obscene songs, while he mixed mortar for the bricklayers.

Joe Wilson's features were extremely Negroid: thick kinky black hair, a broad nose, with dime-size nostrils, heavy lips topped with a mustache and black eyes set far apart. His skin was blackish-brown and coarse—an advantage in fights. Joe Wilson loved to fight, drink and seduce women. He was a real animal; brutal and sadistic.

Under Joe Wilson's influence, Lottie Mae became an indifferent mother. She seldom provided a balanced diet or regular meals for Bobbie, nor was she strict in his bedtime habits. When her caseworker arranged free medical and dental clinic appointments, she frequently ignored them. Lottie Mae rarely supervised Bobbie's play habits and leisure hours, allowing him too much freedom for a boy of elementary school age.

Whenever the caseworker visited Bobbie at school,

6

he had ready answers for her probing questions. He was becoming aware of his unique situation.

The caseworker was suspicious of poor home supervision and care, but Bobbie would always get to school in passable condition; never with the abused, neglected child look. He knew his condition reflected on his mother, and he felt protective towards her.

Lottie Mae's caseworker from the County Welfare Department was Martha Kelly, a veteran social worker of twenty years. She favored the ideas of the "old school" of social work, and didn't agree with the new, benevolent trend in social welfare. Martha Kelly believed in setting these lazy women straight, making them observe welfare rules. She believed that only the "really poor" should be getting help.

Martha Kelly should have been a man. She was solidly built with thick arms and a barrel chest. If she had been a man, she would probably have played football at guard or tackle. She would have been an excellent lineman; rough and aggressive. She had a short, square nose, square chin and a ruddy, freckled complexion which added to the effect of the broad face and short, thick neck and medium height. Martha Kelly presented a formidable obstacle to her "lazy" clients. They couldn't get through or around her. She always stopped them short—a strict "den mother."

Martha Kelly visited Bobbie once a month at school. She would time her visits to coincide with his recess period and talk to Bobbie in the empty classroom, while his classmates were in the schoolyard.

"How are you, Bobbie?" Miss Kelly said.

"Jes fine, Miss Kelly," Bobbie answered.

"You look very nice today."

"Always come t' school lookin' nice."

"Your teacher told me you haven't been alert in class. Haven't you been getting to bed early enough?" A frank stare of suspicion. "Maybe a little too much television?"

Looking at his dusty shoes; "No, mam!"

"Do you stay out late at night?"

"No, mam!"

Sensing Bobbie's reserve, Martha Kelly changed the subject to a lighter vein.

"Your teacher tells me you're helping Mrs. Dodson organize a basketball team to play the other elementary schools."

"Yes, mam!" Glad to be off the grill. "We's gonna be the bes' team. I'm gonna be the captain!"

The conversation soon became frustrating to Martha Kelly. She decided to end it. "I'll be back to see you again, Bobbie. Pay better attention in school, and get to bed earlier." She finished the interview by warning Bobbie, "Behave yourself in school, and after school, too!. . . . Good-bye."

Bobbie watched her leave, glad that it was over for now. He disliked Miss Kelly.

Throughout his elementary school years, Bobbie continued to enjoy exceptional freedom, roaming the streets at will and returning home late at night. He was acquiring the attitudes and habits of the older boys. Bobbie was building a questionable "street" knowledge, enabling him to mature beyond his years and size.

Bobbie may have been on the small, wiry side and below average for his age group but he soon learned to make up for his size. He became alert, aggressive and sensitive to another boy's weaknesses or strengths.

By the sixth and final elementary grade, he was developing into a youthful dictator. His small group of devoted followers fed his ego daily. He loved the way they literally "fell over" themselves obeying his commands.

"Hey, Larry," Bobbie shouted to Larry Johnson. "Ask yo' momma fo' a quarter," he commanded with a confident voice.

"Aw, . . . Bobbie," Larry whined, "My momma won't give me no quarter." With an appeasing tone to his voice, he asked, "Ask fo' a dime, . . . okay?"

Bobbie replied, "Okay. Get the dime. I needs some cake. I'm hungry!" Smiling, he watched the eager disciple obey his request. He was pleased with himself and his ability to use his "friends."

In Bobbie's arsenal of defense tactics, his most prized weapon was the bluff which he could master at will. This faked toughness made up for his lack of real inner courage. He kept his high social position among the street urchins by this ability to outbluff a challenger.

Bobbie was leading the group and carrying the basketball, when they walked into the biggest and best yard in the neighborhood for basketball practice. They were stopped by an unfriendly youth. Standing in front of them was Lorenzo Carr, who was also a sixth grader. He told them to get out of his yard.

Bobbie puffed out his chest, looked over his shoulder and gave the group the "eyeball" signal; then said in a loud voice, "What ya mean? Ain't gonna let my team in yo' yard!" Trying to sound tougher, he added, "Slap ya silly, boy!"

"Ain't movin'. . . . Ain't playin' here. . . . Get out!" commanded Lorenzo Carr, with a voice that cracked, while he rubbed his long brown fingers against his long thighs. Lorenzo Carr was extremely tall for his age.

Bobbie threw the basketball at him with a chest high

thrust. This was the signal to the others. They swarmed over him, punching, kicking and slapping. Lorenzo Carr ran into his house crying.

"What we do now?" asked a worried disciple, sensing the uneasy quiet of the others.

"Don't do nothin' but play basketball!" Bobbie replied. "Ain't gonna let no creep tell us what t' do. Don't give a shit, if'n he gets his momma. She can go frig herself!"

With their confidence restored, they enjoyed laughing at Bobbie's obscene statement. Then they played on the forbidden ground, until Lorenzo Carr's mother came home and chased them out with a broom. They left reluctantly. But not before Bobbie led his gang in shouting obscene insults.

CHAPTER 2

It was the last day of school and it was as hot as a blast furnace; a most unusual, early summer day. The children stayed the required morning hours, received their report cards and with mixed emotions, tramped noisily out of the building. Their teachers followed shortly, eager for a summer's rest.

Joan Harris, the sixth grade teacher, was always the last teacher to leave the school building. The last day was no exception. She turned in her room keys to the school secretary, and preferring not to leave without saying good-bye to Mr. Mathews, rapped politely on his door. The principal's reply cut short the hurried attempt to repair her vanity. She had to walk in his office with blonde strands hanging loosely at her temples, black suit jacket unbuttoned and her makeup—nonexistent. The pink-white skin reflected a ghostly pallor. Her stubby nose was shiny and wrinkled in embarrassment.

In Mr. Mathews' office she breathed a weary sigh, exclaiming that another year of Bobbie Lee, and she would be ready for the old age home. The principal agreed with Miss Harris, and justified their combined decision to promote Bobbie. He stated that another year in sixth grade would have been harmful to both Bobbie and the school. Miss Harris felt a guilty twinge, but agreed verbally with Mr. Mathews.

"It's going to be peaceful, without that boy," Phillip Mathews said, leaned back in his chair and rubbed his left hand over his straight, dull-brown hair. It was thinning rapidly. He was concerned with the rate. "I was getting tired of his face," he confessed and brushed three strands of hair off his left hand. He watched them fall.

Joan Harris wrinkled her nose. "Peaceful? I won't know what to do! I'll be so calm! All my nerves back to normal. I'll be able to teach a decent unit again!" She unwrinkled her nose and waited for the reply.

"Be good for the school, too! Recall how many times I expelled him?" His large brown eyes became slits. His face creased with the question.

She grinned, feeling ill at ease and replied, "Tell the truth, I lost count by Easter."

Phillip Mathews stared at his bruised thumb for about five seconds, thinking to himself, "That damn hammer!" The injury had resulted from a do-it-yourself repair attempt. He quickly returned to the conversation, picked up the word, truth, and said, "Now that you mentioned the word, truth, I keep getting the feeling we didn't reach him." He continued, a serious expression on his face; "We failed that boy." He paused for five full seconds, then said, "All the years he was here. We didn't do anything for him. We really didn't!" He rubbed his head again, and watched three more strands of hair glide to the floor.

"How could we?" asked Joan Harris. She crinkled her stubby nose and continued, "His mother seldom came in even when you sent notes." She paused, brushed her falling locks into place and said with a tense, soft voice, "Even the social worker was disgusted with her." Her pale gray eyes shifted over the numerous papers, books and folders on Mr. Mathews' cluttered desk.

"Couldn't call her the epitome of cooperation, could you?" Phillip Mathews asked. A wry smile crossed his long, thin face, and not expecting an answer, he changed the subject. "Made any progress on that hospital job?"

"Oh, I've got it! Start Monday."

"Glad to hear that!"

The conversation continued in this more pleasant vein. The unpleasant thoughts about Bobbie Lee were forgotten. He was just another problem student promoted purposely to ease the tension in their school.

From this elementary school located in a slum, Bobbie Lee was promoted to a junior high school in a similar neighborhood. Its pupils presented the same type of behavior problems and being older, were more difficult to discipline and control. The results were a tense, rigid school with poor students and little time for teaching.

To Bobbie it was going to be a new life situation. He tried to look into the future, but became even more confused. Bobbie was unable to plan his role. He only had a hazy idea of what to expect; a result of conversations with older boys in his neighborhood.

He wondered about keeping control of his gang. Would he be separated from them, and have to make a new social conquest? Would he be able to outbluff the boys from the other neighborhoods?

Bobbie was from an area in Mercerton known as South Mercerton, and realized he would be meeting some rough characters from the locally notorious slum area—East Mercerton. Since he had about as much real courage as a rabbit, the unpleasant thoughts made him flee the apartment and look for his friends.

Bobbie found his four youthful disciples on the steps of the vacant elementary school, closed for the summer recess. The four youths rose together as if to stand in a military inspection and shouted greetings, almost in unison. Bobbie accepted this hail-to-the-chief with a big smile.

He returned a more quiet, general greeting that had to be shared equally.

"What we gonna do?" Junior McVeigh asked.

"Yeah, what's happenin'?" the other three chimed together.

Bobbie paused, thought for a few seconds, then announced; "I knows what! Let's make it t' the club. We'll tie up the pool table!"

"S . . . S . . . Sounds real good," stuttered Jimmie Heywood, the gang's smallest member. He was eager to get started. His eyes blinked rapidly, and he rubbed his hands nervously.

Remembering past trouble at the club, Calvin, the tallest of the gang, expressed his concern. "Had t' give up the pool table when Mr. Ross foun' out we'd been hoggin' it."

"Think I'm 'fraid of that ugly lookin' ape!" Bobbie retorted.

"I knows ya ain't," Calvin replied. "Might get kicked out fo' good."

"Let me handle that mammy-jammin' fink. Com'on, let's go." Bobbie urged them to follow with a hand waving gesture.

They followed Bobbie's lead and fell in, along side his jaunty step, looking forward to a good time at the club.

The Youth Club was their hangout. It was a local branch of a national service organization, and its purpose was to help boys stay out of trouble.

Classes in art and craft work were part of the club's recreation and character building program. During the classes, discipline was relaxed, providing a democratic classroom to increase learning. The meaning of the word, democracy, was unknown to Bobbie's gang but they got used to the relaxed discipline and took advantage of it.

Bobbie leaned over his painting and whispered, "Hey, Larry, Miss Jensen ain't lookin'." He pointed to the intent young artist on Larry's right and whispered a command, "Mess-up that creep's paper."

Larry smeared the solid-blue sky with three brush strokes of black. It was nothing but noise after that for the rest of the art period. The gang had a good time, laughing and jeering.

Basketball was played in the gym on the third floor. The ceiling was too low and the court, narrow and short. This postage stamp-size basketball court caused many body contacts during a regulation game with ten players.

The basketball games were supposed to inspire teamwork and sportsmanship. But with Bobbie's team the principles of sportsmanship were usually forgotten. They never played a game without making a lot of fouls; elbows placed rudely in opponents' stomachs, arm slaps, tripping, pushing and holding.

If the referee calls were against Bobbie's team, the game usually ended in protest with threats at the other players.

"Foul!" protested Junior McVeigh.

"He pushed Junior!" Bobbie shouted in the referee's face.

The referee shouted at the sweaty, smelly players, "Foul on number three, McVeigh. Two shots for number six!"

They made two lines along the foul line markings. Bobbie leaned closer to the player on his right and whispered, "Don't be walkin' home alone t'night."

Junior McVeigh, on the other side of the same player,

leaned to his left and said, "Gonna lay my fist up-side yo' big head!"

By the end of the third quarter, most of the other players were too scared to play their best game. Bobbie's team won easily that night. They celebrated by stealing donuts from a parked bakery truck and had a pastry feast. It was a double celebration. They had won the game and the league championship for the year.

Bobbie was the leader of the gang. All were Negroes. All were from his section of the city. They were all under his influence, obeying his commands and whims; none of them willing to challenge his position as leader.

Little Jimmie Heywood was the court jester of the group. With his extended ears and wide, monkey-shaped face he would usually ease a tense moment with wise-cracks. His admiration for Bobbie was real, and he was similar to him in size with his small, thin, light-weight body. Jimmie was nervous and jumpy and easily the fastest runner in the gang. When he spoke, he would blink his black eyes rapidly and usually stuttered on the first word.

John Junior McVeigh was the one with the most nerve. He was of dull-normal intelligence, and took his cues from Bobbie. His broad, squat features and beady black eyes gave his face an ugly, sinister effect and his thick hair, matted and kinky and small, pointed ears added to the effect.

Larry Johnson was known as the Hawk; with his dark, bird-like features, beaked nose and high cheek bones. He was effective despite his skinny arms and small fists, and was handy with a brick or a bottle. Dirty street fighting was his favorite pastime. He loved a good gang fight.

Bobbie relied heavily on Calvin Armstrong. He was

16

the biggest member in the gang. Because of his broad, flat head, he was often called Flattop. His facial features matched his head; flat face, broad nose and wide, heavy lips, Calvin may have been unattractive, but he was dependable and had the only real, solid courage. He never bothered to bluff and was strong, well-built, capable of taking as well as giving punishment.

Calvin was content to let Bobbie lead the group. He was the natural first mate, and would rather follow than lead. Calvin was good strong support for the brassy, bantam leader. Bobbie understood Calvin, and used him to his advantage.

Bobbie kept the group together. He gave force, direction and purpose to the group's activities.

Bobbie was small built. And his short, narrow neck, supporting his large watermelon-shaped head made him look awkward. It was too big for his thin frame, narrow shoulders, slender arms and short, slim legs.

His face was oval-shaped with attractive features; a long thin nose with narrow, firm nostrils and bow-shaped lips. He had a brown complexion, black curly-kinky hair and ears that were pasted to his head. Bobbie looked like his mother, except for his darker skin.

CHAPTER 3

It was a chilly, damp and dark November day with slate gray cloud cover; especially gloomy for two Eastern Seaboard residents, a Negro youth and a white adult.

In the disciplinarian's room the hissing radiator seemed to be making fun of the youth and the adult, silently facing each other. The quiet was a change from the loud scene a moment ago.

Rodney Russ had been quietly thinking about the right approach to use to get out of taking his wife to the teachers convention. He had already made plans to attend with two other male teacher friends. and was looking forward to the parties.

He considered himself a "lady killer" and never passed a mirror without glancing at his reflection. At forty, he still considered himself good-looking and was still a bachelor at heart. He was six-three and well preserved, without any middle age spread and his broad shoulders, narrow waist, long arms and legs indicated a swimmers build. He had black hair, prominent forehead and jaw, straight nose, blue eyes, thin lips and soft skin like a woman. Only one odd feature—his ears—they were too small and delicate. He was sensitive about them.

Wild screams shook Rodney Russ out of his daydreaming. He returned to earth and ran from desk to door in time to collide with a flying body. The youth had escaped from the teacher and ran head-on into him.

Mr. Russ kept the boy, sent the teacher back to his class and began the questioning session.

"Mr. DeFrank told me his side. Let's hear your side," Mr. Russ asked, raising his right hand and pointing a long index finger at Bobbie.

Silence . . . from Bobbie Lee.

"I'm giving you a chance," Mr. Russ said, jabbing at the air with his right index finger.

Bobbie raised his head a trifle; just enough for a glance at Mr. Russ, then rolled his eyes downward with arrogant silence.

"Don't roll your eyes at me! Either you tell me what happened, or I'll march you down to the principal's office right now!" Mr. Russ was almost shouting now. "You've got one minute, boy!" He tapped three times on his desk blotter with his favorite finger.

Fifty-five seconds of silence, and then mumbling.

"Don't mumble. Can't hear you."

"That Charles Carter, tried t' be bad. Talkin' 'bout my momma. Askin' me, where's my daddy?"

Mr. Russ interrupted, "So, that gave you the right to throw a book at him?" He pointed once and tapped once.

"No."

"Why did you do it?"

"Ain't gonna get 'way with that nasty talk!"

"Alright, go on." He glanced at the clock.

"After I threw the book, Mr. DeFrank grabbed my shirt collar. Yanked me out my seat." Bobbie leaned forward on the chair and shouted, "Don't like nobody touchin' on me! Tol him off!"

"Was that right? Talking back to your teacher." The index finger was held aloft, waiting for the reply.

"Ain't gonna put his hands on me!" Tears blurred his sight. "Nobody's gonna put his hands on me!"

"Don't you worry about anybody putting their hands

19

on you! Did you threaten Mr. DeFrank?" The index finger
became airborne again.

Bobbie jumped off the chair and shouted, "Tol' him I'd hit
him with a chair, if'n he didn't take his hands off me!"

Bobbie didn't know the principal was standing behind
him, when he shouted the last sentence. That was enough for
the principal's tender ears.

He sent Bobbie home with a sealed envelope, explaining
what had happened and ordered Bobbie not to return to school
without his mother. Bobbie wuietly handed the note to his
mother, who struggled through it. She looked at him, pouted
and asked, "Why, Bobbie?"

"Don't like 'em talkin' nasty."

"Don't listen. What you care, they tell ies 'bout me!" She
bit her lower lip, and winced from the sting.

"Can't help it, momma. Get mad inside!"

"Listen t' me. Tell 'em yo' daddy's down Alabama. Don't
need him up here, 'cause yo' momma takes care of ya."

He hugged his mother, laid his head on her shoulder and
asked, "Takin' me back?"

"After we eats, we's both goin' back." She drew in her
lower lip again and bit it, lightly.

The trip back to school was quiet. Bobbie was content to
walk silently beside his mother, and tried to remember the last
time his mother had been to school. It was somewhere back in
that almost forgotten part of his life—elementary school.

His mother's thoughts were back at the apartment. She
wondered about Joe Wilson. Would he stop over while she
was out? He usually did stop in the afternoon when he
wasn't working. She knew he became angry, when he didn't
find her home. It made her feel uneasy.

He was suspicious and jealous of her and became violent when mad. Lottie Mae fought the uneasy feeling, telling herself he would have to wait. She could explain, when she got back. Lottie Mae looked at Bobbie and ordered, "Don't make no mo' trouble, when we's talkin' t' the principal. Hear me?"

"Yes, momma."

The secretary ushered them into the principal's office, and told them to be seated. The principal would be along shortly.

They sat down cautiously as if expecting something to be on their chairs, and waited silently for the principal.

Bobbie broke the silence. "Got a feelin', I'm gonna be expelled." His voice was high, almost squeaking. "Principal don't like me. Bet he talked t' Mr. Russ. Mr. De-Frank, too!"

The sudden sight of Mr. Flossman was startling. Harold Flossman was fifty, bald and wore thick, black, horn-rimmed eyeglasses. He had a round, shiny nose that stuck out between thick, convex lenses which made his brown eyes look like huge circles. He was a comical sight, but his staff never laughed at him. Harold Flossman was the principal and let everyone know it. He sensed the effect his entrance had made, and quickly took charge of the meeting.

"You are fully aware of the incident your boy was involved in today, Mrs. Lee?" Mr. Flossman lisped.

"Miss Lee."

"Oh, I'm sorry, Miss Lee!" Mr. Flossman replied. He hesitated, then said, "In view of the threats he made and the book that was thrown, you couldn't judge the punishment too severe, if I expelled your son for one week, could you?" He lisped all "th" sounds.

The sudden, blunt statement was too much for Lottie

Mae. It was awhile, before she could mumble her answer. "If that's what ya want." She pouted and stared at the floor.

Mr. Flossman countered, "His behavior was incorrigible! If we allowed such actions to continue, the whole school would be in a state of bedlam!"

While Mr. Flossman was talking, Lottie Mae decided she didn't like him, and the way he talked to her. Aware that he finished speaking and was waiting for an answer, she came to another conclusion. It was no use arguing with this man. She answered, "I knows ya got rules. I knows they has t' be followed." She paused, then said, "What ya do . . . alright with me." She lapsed into silence and pouted.

Mr. Flossman sensed the woman's dislike but didn't really care. He had reached his limit, putting up with hoodlum students and parents that did not care how their children behaved. How could he run a school with such pupils? "I need lion tamers not teachers!" Mr. Flossman said to himself.

Aware that a lapse had occurred and a decision was necessary, he decided to stall. He turned to Bobbie and lisped, "Well, young man, do you have anything to add to this conversation?"

"No, sir!"

Mr. Flossman glanced at the clock. He was past his pre-allotted time for this meeting. He decided to end the interview.

"In view of all the circumstances, I can't do anything else, but expel your son for one week," Mr. Flossman stated and looked directly at Lottie Mae. "And furthermore, while he's on suspension, he's not to be allowed out of the house during school hours." He stared at Bobbie, "You understand young man? You must stay at home during school hours?" Without waiting for an answer, he glanced at the clock again and continued, "Are there any questions, Miss Lee?" His lisp was getting worse.

It was obvious to Lottie Mae, he didn't want any questions, so she answered, "No."

"That's all. Thank you and good-bye," Mr. Flossman lisped, with a pleased look on his face. Smirking, he watched them leave.

Lottie Mae felt a sudden, chilling breeze and pulled her cloth coat collar around her throat.

Bobbie looked at his mother, followed her move and asked, "Think maybe it's gonna snow?"

She glanced at the sky. "Looks more like rain. Not cold 'nough fo' snow. Com'on, let's hurry."

"Momma, do I got t' stay inside?"

She thought about the principal's command and decided that it was not what he said, but the sassy way he said it. She thought, "Hopes all school principals ain't like him." Lottie Mae remembered Bobbie's question. She looked down at Bobbie and said, "Maybe I'll let ya out, if ya promise t' behave yo'self."

Lottie Mae began thinking about Joe Wilson and about Bobbie being home all next week. She knew Joe didn't like having Bobbie around. After a few minutes, she decided; "When Joe comes over, I'll let Bobbie go t' the movies o' somethin'." Having made her decision, she retreated into her shell and walked home in complete silence.

Bobbie wondered about his mother's silence but was content just to be with her. He kept quiet the rest of the way home.

CHAPTER 4

The weekend had been enjoyable for Bobbie and his gang. Spending Saturday at the Youth Club, they had won four dollars playing pool. The gambling was played under the act of just-for-fun games.

Calvin was the best pool player in the group. His favorite game was eight ball and he seldom lost. He loved to show-off his skill on hard combination shots. Bobbie made good use of Calvin's playing skill, and used him as the team's anchor man. The ideal position after the opposing "pigeons" have been "setup" for higher stakes.

The group's winnings would be spent group style; cakes and soda for all. If the money held out, they would go for seconds on everything. It was not every day that a "killing" was made.

This particular Saturday had been a banner day at the green table with the small ivory spheres behaving themselves splendidly. They lost the right amount of games before the friendly game became a last-one-for-money contest. Bobbie and Calvin played the two unsuspecting "patsies." The four smiling faces became serious and intent, after Calvin scattered the racked balls.

It was a good scatter, with the three ball plopping into the left corner pocket. Calvin chalked his cue stick, looked the balls over and saw a natural combination shot for the right corner pocket with a good after-shot position. Leaning over the table, he called his shot. "One ball. Right co'ner pocket." He pointed his cue stick at the named pocket. "Off the seven ball."

The one ball dropped into the correct pocket, the cue ball stopped in the right place and the next shot was obvious to everyone, especially the two, frowning opponents. Calvin sunk the seven ball easily.

Calvin leaned on the cushion, eyed the angle of the next combination shot. He would have to bank the four ball off the cushion to hit the two ball, which was being blocked from a straight shot by the six and twelve balls. Calvin looked at Bobbie. "Think it'll go?"

Bluffing as usual Bobbie shouted, "Go 'head man. Make it!"

Calvin made that shot and went on to clear the table of the four, five and six balls.

The game winning ball is the eight ball. If a player should scratch, while trying to sink it, he would lose the game in spite of having sunk all of the required balls. A scratch can be caused by sinking the cue ball in a pocket, or failing to hit the eight ball with the cue ball. The game could also be lost by sinking the eight ball in an unnamed pocket, or failure to name the chosen pocket. With all this in mind, Calvin checked the eight ball against the cue ball's position.

The tension was mounting. Bobbie played it "cool" and kept silent. Little Jimmie's face was serious, minus the court jester smile and usual laughing taunts. Junior and Larry glanced at each other without comment.

Both opponents were amazed. They never expected such good pool playing.

"Eight ball. Lef' co'ner." Calvin bent over the table, aimed for a full twenty seconds before he shot. The cue ball smacked the eight ball, and sent it spinning to the left corner pocket. It rammed against the leather-edged pocket and plopped in noisily.

Junior and Larry broke into a cheer. Bobbie gave Calvin a hug, and the others gathered around laughing and talking. With a broad, white-toothed smile, Calvin collected a dollar each from the two losers. Grinning, he asked, "Try again?"

The challenge was accepted, but with one change. They would break first which is an unusual privilege for losers to get in a pool game.

The second game lasted a little longer. The losers broke first and Bobbie shot first for his side. But once Calvin chalked his cue and aimed for his first shot, the game was decided quickly in the gang's favor.

With the "loot" in their pockets, they left and celebrated at Hal's Candy Store next to the club. It was cake and soda for everybody.

A half-hour later, they stepped off the store's worn, stone steps with full stomachs and crossed Main Street. With their cocky struts, they spread over the entire sidewalk, forcing opposite pedestrian traffic into the gutters. They were a contented group.

"T . . . T . . . That's the easiest money we ever got!" Jimmie said to the others.

Bobbie answered for everybody. "Sho beats shinin' shoes!"

Larry seconded the motion. "Man, it sho do!"

Junior McVeigh just nodded in agreement. He was too full of cake and soda to bother talking.

Jimmie stopped the group. His smiling face changed to a stupid, amazed look; mimicking the faces on the two losers.

Laughing and gloating, they enjoyed the feeling of having fooled someone out of their money. Working for money would soon become old stuff; they had found one of the easier ways.

They separated where Ridge Street dips under railroad tracks and the freeway, promising to meet there at 1:00 p.m. on Sunday. They agreed that the Regent Theater was the best place to spend Sunday afternoon. It was showing the usual horror and science fiction movies.

Bobbie lived the farthest from the club on Alliance Street, near a Jewish synagogue and a colored bar.

The synagogue was the symbol of the old status, while the bar was the symbol of the street's new status.

Bobbie liked the bar. It was a good place for shining shoes. The customers were always well-dressed and reserved. That was the only type of customer Fats Roy wanted at his place. He always welcomed outsiders (whites) and ran a quiet, intimate lounge. "Hip" whites and local political celebrities visited the bar, as well as the "hip" colored crowd. Roy was proud of his juke box. He kept it well-stocked with the best in modern jazz and kept it playing continually, even at bar expense.

Bobbie admired the neatly dressed "cats" in the bar. He would listen to every word and watch every gesture, while shining a customer's shoes.

He lived two houses from Roy's bar in a three story, red brick, semidetached house that was now an apartment dwelling. His mother's apartment was on the third floor. It was connected to the second floor by a worn, wooden staircase. The railing had missing spokes and a dirty, grimy finish and the hallway was covered with wallpaper patches. Sections were faded, dirty and covered with crayon marks. It was a dark staircase. The light bulbs had been broken and never replaced.

Bobbie climbed the stairs rapidly for the first two

landings but walked the last set of stairs at a much slower pace. He stepped quietly into the kitchen. Bobbie had learned from experience to enter the apartment quietly.

He was only a few steps inside the cluttered kitchen, when he heard voices coming from the living room; the front of the apartment, which also was his bedroom at night.

"Com'on, baby. Be nice."

"No! wait 'til t'night."

"Gonna get drunk t'night, baby."

"Don't care."

"Baby, I'm feelin' sharp, now!"

The voices stopped, but Bobbie could hear movement on the couch. After a short interval, a pleading voice came through the doorway. "Com'on, baby. Need a little right now. Not t'night!" More movement; then just the rhythmic, muted sound of an old, familiar act.

Tears streaming down his face, Bobbie walked quickly out of the kitchen and down the stairs. He sat on the top step of the first floor landing, laid his head on his arms and sobbed, softly, for a long time.

Glad that no one saw or heard him, Bobbie dried his face on his shirt sleeve and walked out of the building. He felt better. But he still wanted to walk off the hurt feeling, before entering the apartment again. He also wanted to allow enough time for that man to leave. Bobbie guessed that the man was Joe Wilson, who was with his mother often now. Bobbie didn't like him and knew Joe Wilson felt the same towards him. Bobbie avoided him, when he was drunk. "Wilson is a mean bastard, when he's high!" thought Bobbie, as he walked past the last Jewish delicatessen in the neighborhood; operated by an old die-hard, who had refused to move away.

When Bobbie returned to the apartment, he was glad
to find his mother alone. He noticed her hand was still on
the telephone receiver, and guessed that she had just
finished making arrangements for him to stay someplace.

Lottie Mae lived for her weekends. She would arrange
overnight visits for Bobbie to stay at an aunt, or a friend's
house for Saturday night and the recovery period; Sunday
morning. Sunday afternoon was managed easily by sending him to the movies. Out of the way, Bobbie would not
spoil her weekend spree, or get her boyfriend mad. She
knew Joe Wilson didn't like Bobbie.

Lottie Mae prepared Saturday's supper early, served
Bobbie and then, quietly told him about his overnight
stay with Aunt Julie Armstrong on Morrow Street. Bobbie had learned to expect these weekend trips as routine,
accepted them without asking questions. Besides, he liked
Aunt Julie. Actually, she wasn't his aunt. It was just that
Bobbie liked to call her, aunt. He always felt at ease with
her, and since she was an elderly woman, the title came
naturally. She was enjoyable company, and had a very
nice way of making a young boy feel at home; at the same
time feel important.

Carrying his cloth, overnight bag, Bobbie walked the
few blocks to Aunt Julie's house and knocked on the unpainted wood door. After a short wait, the door opened
slowly and a wrinkled face peered around it.

"Hi, Bobbie. Come on in!" greeted Aunt Julie. She
put her thin arm around his shoulders and smiled, revealing toothless gums. Aunt Julie had given up trying to get
used to her false teeth a long time ago.

Enjoying the friendly greeting, Bobbie replied, "Thank
you, Aunt Julie." He smiled and his eyes brightened.

There was plenty of attention and affection handed
out during a Saturday night stay at Aunt Julie's. It usually

began with a snack; milk and cake, and then questions on Bobbie's welfare and school work.

"Tell me what happen, Bobbie," asked Aunt Julie. Her rimless eyeglasses hung on the end of her small flat nose, which was attached to a brown-skinned face. The wrinkled skin was like old, dry leather.

Sensing real interest, Bobbie told about the trouble in school, including the return visit to the principal's office. He enjoyed every word of it. And Aunt Julie, who loved gossip, listened to every word. She filed every detail into the current events department of her brain for her weekly report over the neighborhood gossip network.

The story completed, Bobbie waited respectfully for Aunt Julie's wise comment.

It came quickly. She removed her eyeglasses, rubbed her tired eyes and summed the whole matter up in one breath.

"That principal is a stinker! Just plain mean and nasty. Expellin' you. Not doin' nothin' to that other boy!" She banged the edge of the formica-topped kitchen table with her small fist for emphasis. Her dull black eyes widened into a fiery look.

After Saturday night's pleasant visit, Bobbie went to Mass with Aunt Julie on Sunday morning, even though he was not Catholic. Aunt Julie was one of a few Negro Catholics in South Mercerton and liked to take Bobbie to church. She knew his mother never took him to church or gave him any religious training. This upset her. She was a strict Catholic.

Bobbie left Aunt Julie's house after lunch. He met the gang under the freeway overpass at 1:00 p.m. They hurried uptown to the Regent Theater, looking forward to an afternoon's enjoyment.

It was nearly 5:00 p.m. when the Regent Theater

ushers opened the side door to let the bleary eyed audience out. The sudden light made their eyes blink. Bobbie and his gang had just spent over three hours in the theater's darkness. They had watched two feature films; a horror movie about dead people rising out of coffins and a more modern, end-of-the-world, science fiction movie. Both movies were enjoyable to their young minds.

They had walked only a short distance down the steep incline of Enterprise Street, when Bobbie spotted Charles Carter, across the street. Carter was with two friends. Bobbie figured that five against three were good odds, and decided not to lose the chance for revenge. He gave the field command. The group spread out and marched across the street. They circled the surprised enemy in front of a window display, showing the latest fashions in ladies' shoes.

"Where ya goin', boy?" asked Bobbie in a forced, gruff tone of voice. He felt the blood rushing to his head and a strange feeling in his stomach.

"None of yo' mother-humpin' business, faggot," answered Charles Carter, trying to sound as brave as possible, while his black, scared eyes counted Bobbie's gang. Carter stood with his long feet apart, large hands on narrow hips and closely shaved head tilted slightly to his right side. His jaw was opening and closing, if he wanted to speak. But he said nothing.

This show of toughness was all Bobbie needed. He gave the signal to Junior McVeigh, who grabbed Carter around the neck. They grappled against the window, puffing their breaths on each other. Junior managed to release Carter's neck and pin both arms behind his back. With Charles Carter helpless, and the other two boys kept at bay; Bobbie began punching him in the stomach, then started hitting him in the face and head. When Bobbie became tired, he stopped. Junior let the battered boy slump to the concrete.

Resting on his knees, Charles Carter covered his face for protection, expecting more punches. When they didn't come, he looked up and saw Bobbie's face. Words came out of that face with heavy breathing:

"If'n I ever . . . hear yo' dirty mouth . . . say nasty things . . . 'bout my momma . . . 'gain . . . beat on ya . . . so bad . . . won't never . . . talk . . . 'bout nobody's momma . . . 'gain!"

Charles Carter didn't answer.

"Hear me? Ya black ape!" Bobbie shouted, his eyes growing larger.

Charles Carter looked up. "I hears ya."

"Get up! Get yo' black ass outta here!"

They watched the three youths disappear around the corner of Enterprise and Freedom Streets.

Calvin turned towards Bobbie and asked, "Think he's gonna make trouble?"

"Don't give a shit 'bout him. No how!" Bobbie was still enjoying the feeling of having gotten back at Charles Carter. It made him feel good inside.

During the rest of the walk home, Bobbie was a part of the usual, after movie chatter, but his mind was on Charles Carter.

"Never can tell. Might meet Carter. Gonna be lookin' for me, now. Got t' be lookin' out fo' him."

Preferring not to think about it, since it made him feel uneasy, he shut the thoughts out of his mind. Bobbie turned to Jimmy and asked, "What cha do, when them ghosts popped out of the coffins?" Not waiting for an answer, he asked, "Bet ya was scared?"

CHAPTER 5

Bobbie was glad to find his mother alone, sober and not moodily abrupt with a hangover. He knew she was in a good mood from the friendly inquiry. "Hi, Bobbie. Like the movies?" asked Lottie Mae.

"Sho did, momma!" answered Bobbie, smiling.

"That's good. Hungry?"

"Starved!" He rubbed his stomach for emphasis.

"Sit down. Fix ya some supper."

Bobbie was hungry and gobbled forkfuls of meat and potatoes and enjoyed his mother's company. She seldom sat with him, while he ate. Taking advantage of it, he told her about both movies, between mouthfuls. He enjoyed telling about the ghosts and monsters in the horror movie and the wierd-looking Martians in the science fiction movie. It was a rare moment, having his mother alone; not sharing her company with Joe Wilson.

The change from the enjoyable meal with his mother to being alone in his dark bedroom was a burden. Bobbie couldn't fall asleep. He tossed continuously during most of the night, disturbed by the day's encounter with Charles Carter and the thought of being home alone for a week. The idea of empty days without friends, was too persistent to shut out of his mind. He was uneasy; much too uneasy to sleep.

Monday morning passed without incident. The boredom reached its peak by mid-afternoon, then relieved by a trip to the Youth Club. Being the first one in the recreation room, Bobbie racked the pool balls and played a game of rotation. One game passed into three, before the gang arrived. Jimmie, Larry and Junior walked into the game room, shouting greetings.

Calvin was last. He walked in slowly and greeted Bobbie quietly. After waiting a moment, Calvin leaned toward Bobbie. "Talkin' t' Tommy Bethea, Charles Carter ain't gonna tell the principal 'bout Sunday." He picked up the blue, cue stick chalk with his right hand and stared at it. "Carter tol' Tommy, got plen'y time t' get even."

Larry Johnson came over and deposited his feelings. "Maybe we shouldn't of beat on him so bad, Bobbie!" His voice, climbing an octave higher in pitch; "Carter got lotsa tough friends!" The tip of his nose moved up and down, while he spoke.

Bobbie looked at their faces. They looked worried. He decided to do something about it. Standing as tall as he could and lifting his chin for effect, Bobbie shouted as loud as he could; "Charles Carter ain't shit! His black ass belongs t' me!" He pointed at himself with his left index finger. "Anytime he wants t' get even, go 'head an' try! Beat him once. Can do it again!" His eyes looked like two black agates.

Bobbie continued with his high-pitched squeaking voice, "Tell Bethea, Calvin." Before the last word echoed off the smooth, plastered walls, he began feeling the challenge rise within him, unable to stop himself he made another boast, "Ever catch Carter 'round here, gonna beat on him bad!"

Contrasting Bobbie's excited voice, Calvin asked at a more subdued level, "All that?"

"Don't worry none. Tell him. Charles Carter ain't shit!" Bobbie repeated for effect with bulbous black eyes.

The speech made no real headway. If Bobbie planned

34

to raise their spirits, he failed. The others didn't feel quite up to Bobbie's level of confidence. They kept silent with serious expressions and glanced uneasily at each other.

The following morning found Bobbie trudging on an empty stomach to the grocery store; a half-block from his house. He had gotten up before his mother, and found the kitchen just about empty of food. Not wanting to disturb her, he decided to get some cereal and milk at Jake's store and put it on their store bill.

Before Jake Miller would bag the two items, he made Bobbie listen to a lecture about his mother's irregular payments towards her food bill.

"Make sure you tell your mother. You hear?" Jake said, spitting out the words. "Don't mind a few dollars on the bill. Hasn't paid me a cent in over three weeks! What she do with her relief check?" He stared at Bobbie, then squinted his green eyes and said, "Spends it on booze and that boyfriend." Jake rubbed his fat face with short, thick fingers. Then he scratched his bald dome but still no reply from Bobbie.

Bobbie stared rigidly at the brown bag on the counter. He was hungry. He knew he had to control himself. A pause of ten seconds became awkward to both, then Jake broke the tense silence, bellowing at Bobbie. "So, alright! Take it this time! Remember. No more, 'til I get some money."

Bobbie grabbed the bag and flew out of the store.

"Don't forget! Tell your mother!" Jake shouted at Bobbie's back.

Bobbie ran all the way back to the apartment. He couldn't escape quickly enough from the man with the raspy, irritating voice. Bobbie wiped his face again. He could still feel the wet spit on his face, still smell the cigar breath.

He had barely swallowed the last mouthful of corn-

35

flakes, when an unexpected guest arrived; Miss Martha Kelly, the social worker from the County Welfare Department. She made her quarterly visit that morning, a little too early to suit Bobbie. Lottie Mae had to get out of bed and greet her unwelcomed guest. The conversation that followed was typical for the quarterly visit.

"Is this how you keep your place?" asked Martha Kelly. Not waiting for an answer, she continued, "Is this how you take care of your child?" She pointed a menacing right index finger at Bobbie.

"A little tired this mornin', Miss Kelly." Lottie Mae stared at the floor and pouted.

"Too tired from what, Miss Lee?"

"Up late, doin' cho'es." Lottie Mae's pout became more pronounced.

"Give you the benefit of the doubt." Martha Kelly let her voice signal the end to that particular topic.

She focused her hazel eyes on Bobbie and didn't end her stern, lengthy stare until she asked, "What are you doing home?"

"I . . . I . . . I . . . was expelled from school las' Friday."

"You were what?" Martha Kelly opened her case book and flipped the pages noisily.

Lottie Mae interrupted, "Fight at school. Some boy was teasin' him."

"Another fight." Martha Kelly began writing in her casebook.

Bobbie came to his own defense. He retold the complete incident to Miss Kelly, who listened without sitting down. She just stood there, recording and nodding her head, confirming her hearing ability.

After Bobbie finished, she made a decision. "I'll see Mr. DeFrank and Mr. Russ. Mr. Flossman, too. Maybe I'll get you back in school," she said without apparent enthusiasm or confidence and closed her casebook.

Miss Kelly had too many quarterly visits that had to be made that day. She wanted to end this one quickly. Her case load was too large to allow her the luxury of concentrated supervision for any one case. She made an "Inspector-General" tour of the apartment with Lottie Mae trailing behind, so she could point out her failures as a mother and homemaker.

Both Bobbie and Lottie Mae sighed visibly, after Miss Kelly left their cluttered apartment.

Bobbie looked at his mother, with a question spreading across his face. "Momma, is all white ladies like Miss Kelly?"

"Don't think so. Can't all be that bad!"

"Don't like Miss Kelly," Bobbie said. "Should sit an' talk t' us 'stead of pokin' her nose all over the place."

Lottie Mae looked at Bobbie and smiled. Thinking his statement over, she agreed with him and replied, almost in a whisper, "Maybe she should try an' understan' us. Not jes boss us 'round, like a cop." Lottie Mae's voice continued low in volume; almost monotone level. "I'd like somebody . . . outside my life . . . t' talk with."

The last word scarcely had time to fade away, when the familiar, heavy tread of Joe Wilson was recognized by mother and son. A foreboding air filtered up the stairs and into the kitchen, surrounding Lottie Mae and Bobbie. The tension rose steadily. His treading sounds became heavier and closer. The footsteps were awkward.

Bobbie looked at his mother, who put a thin, reassuring hand on his arm. The consoling effect was lost in one glance at the hostile sight in the doorway. Joe Wilson was swaying; the familiar influence of alcohol. He blurted out, "Got money?"

"Money fo' what? Mo' drink?"

"Got money, woman?"

"Not fo' no drink!"

The refusal reached some primeval depth, beneath the thin, civilized veneer of that swaying, dark figure. Primitive instincts rose to the surface, seizing control. The cumbersome, swaying figure stopped, stood still for a moment, then lumbered towards Lottie Mae. Grabbing her throat with almost subhuman strength, Joe Wilson pulled her out of the chair and shouted into her face with his whiskey breath. "Get me money!"

Lottie Mae couldn't answer or protest. She could only make choking sounds and struggled to release the steel-like grip on her throat. His fingers felt like pincers. She couldn't breathe.

Relief came unexpectedly; Bobbie had circled the table and threw himself bodily at the huge hulk of flesh. His bodily thrust mustered barely enough force to throw Joe Wilson off balance, breaking his grip around Lottie Mae's throat.

Joe Wilson turned toward Bobbie and slapped him across his face. Bobbie went stumbling backwards over a chair and landed against the kitchen sink with a hard thump. While Bobbie leaned against the sink, face stinging, head throbbing, Joe Wilson started towards him. Lottie Mae saw in his face a familiar look of hate mixed with pleasure. She threw herself between them screaming, "I'll give ya money!"

Joe Wilson stopped. "Better get it quick, befo' I beat on him bad."

It was a fair exchange. Joe Wilson got his money and in return, he left. When he stumbled out of the kitchen, it seemed as if the apartment were immediately cleansed. His foul whiskey breath left with him.

The morning had been a little too hectic for both parties involved. Lottie Mae decided to visit with Bernice Alliston, leaving Bobbie free to violate school orders during his expelled period. He couldn't stand the apartment, either. As soon as his mother left, Bobbie forgot her orders for him to stay in the apartment. He scampered down the steps and out of the building.

It was city air but it was free of Joe Wilson's whiskey breath. He breathed deeply, expelling the polluted air from his lungs; the air that he had shared with Joe Wilson.

Bobbie could never begin to describe the hate he had for that man, so he never talked about him to his mother or anyone else. He knew she had some kind of attraction for that brutal animal. Bobbie sensed she was also afraid of him. Joe Wilson seemed to have some kind of control over his mother. This bothered him.

These thoughts occupied his mind, while he walked against the gradual incline of Merchant Street. At the intersection of Cooper and Merchant Streets, Bobbie looked up and stared at the barred windows of the Hunts County Jail. He tried to think what it would be like in jail. Bobbie had heard some of his mother's male visitors talk about it and the workhouse. He remembered some of their descriptions. But his young mind couldn't imagine clearly what it would really be like.

Bobbie stepped between two parked cars and was about to cross to the county jail side of Merchant Street, when his foot kicked a large, metal disc. The disc was easily familiar; it was a hub cap from a car wheel. After he picked it up, he remembered that some gas stations pay up to fifty cents for hub caps.

He retraced his footsteps towards the gas stations in the Morrow Street area, hoping for a quick sale. The prospect of spending money helped him forget about the morning and Joe Wilson.

It occurred to Bobbie, this hub cap business could be a quick source of ready cash to finance the group's affairs.

They wouldn't have to find them in the gutters, either. They could be taken off car wheels, very easily, with a screwdriver.

"See what the gang thinks," he decided as he walked along Morrow Street, passed decaying, overcrowded houses. "Maybe we can get some money fas'." Bobbie held the hub cap tightly under his left arm and hurried his pace. He was beginning to feel better, completely forgetting about Joe Wilson.

CHAPTER 6

With little Jimmie Heywood as scout, the gang located a parked, 2-door, '57, Plymouth sedan in a dark, narrow parking lot between two office buildings. The doors had been left unlocked and the locked glove compartment was sprung easily. Calvin concentrated on the hub caps, removing all four with a minimum of noise. Jimmie and Junior McVeigh rifled through the contents of the glove compartment. Larry and Bobbie were lookouts at opposite ends of the parking lot. The operation went smoothly. Everyone did his job quickly, without mistakes or noise.

Jimmie and Junior took thirty-nine cents in change, a screwdriver, pliers, gloves and flashlight from the glove compartment. Calvin wrapped the four hub caps in old, musty burlap and stuffed them into a large, brown paper bag. He put the other items in the bag, also.

The "job" completed, they left individually. Calvin stepped out casually to a deserted Slate Street, walked directly across it onto the pavement in front of the Hotel Mercer. He navigated the few, necessary steps around the corner, then down the steep, narrow incline of Channel Street, holding the innocent-looking, brown bag firmly under his right arm.

Jimmie, empty handed, tiptoed down the brick-paved alley leading to Wilson Street. After checking both directions from the doorway of the state unemployment office, he hurried down Wilson Street, crossed Slate Street and continued down the steep incline of Wilson Street. He turned left at narrow Rampart Street. One block down, he met Calvin at Branch Street. They continued down Branch Street past white and red, brick front houses that were now mostly offices with shutters and multipaned windows, creating an Early American facade.

Junior McVeigh, Bobbie and Larry waited in the alley's protective shadows next to the First Precinct Police Station that faced a dark, deserted Channel Street. Bobbie was confident. Calvin had all the "booty." If stopped by a policeman, they would just be boys that were up too late on a weekday night.

Bobbie relaxed while he waited with his two partners, and when the ten minutes had elapsed, he gave the "go" signal. They moved out individually. Walking abreast, they were silent until they reached Slate Street. Then Bobbie broke the silence; "Let's walk down Slate. Turn at Morrow. Make sho we don't meet Calvin an' Jimmie." The others obeyed without comment or question.

Bobbie's planning was effective. The entry had been successful and everyone got home without getting stopped. Calvin stored everything in a wooden orange crate in his cellar, covering it with piles of newspaper.

Part of the plan was not to meet in the neighborhood but to go straight home. They would get together later in the week, and distribute the loot piecemeal; one hub cap at a time to the many gas stations in the South Mercerton area. The other items would be used or sold. For their parents, it was decided that a soda at Hal's candy store next to the Youth Club would be a good enough reason for getting home late. Since the Youth Club closes at nine, arriving home around ten wouldn't be out of line with their excuse.

"Yeah, ev'rythin' went good!" Bobbie said to himself

42

as he climbed the stairs. He was more than pleased with the night's work. "Jes the beginnin', too!" he murmured to himself, and opened the apartment door.

His mother was asleep. Her head was propped on her arms, resting against the oilcloth covered table. Bobbie walked over to wake her but realized she was in a delicate condition. He left her alone to continue her drunken sleep and went into his bedroom. Bobbie removed his clothes, plopped on the unmade bed and was asleep in hardly more than a minute.

Thursday passed without incident. Bobbie didn't see his gang until Friday afternoon, when he met them in front of the club, and assigned each one an item to sell. Before sending Calvin home for the stolen merchandise, he told them to meet that night in nearby Hurst Alley.

After the loot was sold, they met in Hurst Alley next to an ancient, unpainted, frame garage; formerly used as a horse stable and later as a distillery during prohibition. They wanted to divide the money in privacy. Since it was Friday, Bobbie had decided it was safe to send one hub cap per man out to four separate gas stations. He kept the gloves and tools for their own use and sold the flashlight. The total of the night's work and the day's sales came to two dollars and twenty-five cents; added to the thirty-nine cents from the compartment, the total amount of change looked impressive in Bobbie's hand. After struggling through a fair distribution, they decided it would be better to walk home separately.

Bobbie was elated from the week's success. He strolled leisurely down Collins Street with his share of the change in his left pocket. In spite of the five degree list on his port side, he stayed on course, but never expected to meet Charles Carter with his two friends. They had been searching the neighborhood—for him.

The unexpected meeting happened on Barge Street, because Bobbie had decided to take the long way around to his section of Alliance Street. Not wasting any time, he looked around quickly, then decided; "Have t' make a run fo' it!" Before they could move towards him, Bobbie spun around and started running; the change jingling loudly in his pocket.

Carter and company followed Bobbie, racing up Barge Street, around the corner and down Collins Street, heading toward Ridge Street.

Bobbie knew Charles Carter wouldn't quit the chase, but hoped the other two would tire. He was running faster, breathing easier, by the time he reached Ridge Street. His short legs were pumping hard against the concrete pavement. Bobbie flung himself around the corner into Ridge Street, heading towards the railroad and freeway overpasses and Alliance Street. Curious pedestrians looked at the running boys with questionable glances and stepped aside unwillingly, providing ample space on the narrow sidewalk.

Charles Carter kept looking back, urging more speed out of his rapidly tiring running mates strung out in single file. On Ridge Street, he realized it was just going to be Bobbie and him. It wasn't going according to plan. But he wanted to get Bobbie; this kept his tired leg muscles moving.

Bobbie stopped under the freeway overpass and leaned against the concrete wall. He choked and gagged for breath—almost vomited. Regaining his breath, he noticed some loose bricks. They were good enough for splitting heads. He waited, patiently, for Charles Carter.

It was a short wait. Carter made the turn under the railroad overpass at a slow trot, and didn't stop until he was under the freeway overpass. His tired, damp body came to rest fifty feet from Bobbie. Carter's chest was heaving. Bobbie could hardly understand the hoarse, breathless voice. "Got ya now, Bobbie. . . . Jus' you an' me."

Feeling better, Bobbie answered; "Jes you an' me an' these here bricks." He lifted both bricks for a better view, and didn't wait for a reply. "Keep on comin'. Gonna lay 'em up-side yo' head!"

The bricks were a surprise. Carter looked down at the brick pavement. His section was intact; not a loose brick to save his soul, or stop a bloody massacre. Carter lifted his head, took a deep breath. He opened his mouth as if to speak but didn't; just breathed through it. Bobbie could hear his heavy breathing.

Bobbie said between breaths; "Better fo'get 'bout fightin'. Gonna stan' here 'til ya turn 'round an' get on home." His face was rigid except for his nostrils dilating from the heavy breathing. Bobbie's lips were set in a grim pout. The sweat dried on his temples from the brisk, night air.

Carter retreated without a word. He didn't have the nerve to attempt anything, while Bobbie had the upper hand. Besides, he wanted to give him the same treatment that he got, gang style. Walking slowly up Ridge Street, he voiced his feelings, "Thinks he's so bad! Get his little butt, yet!"

Bobbie watched Charles Carter's strategic withdrawal, then let out a breathy sigh. He regained his wind and started walking slowly up the curving grade of Alliance Street, heading towards his tenement sanctuary.

The worn, dirty steps creaked happily under his dusty shoes. Bobbie laughed to himself on the second landing, when he noticed that he still held the bricks in his hands. He said to himself, "I'll keep 'em. Got me outta a real tight spot!"

The apartment was empty and Bobbie wondered about his mother's absence. He went into the living room which also served as his bedroom, and put the bricks, lovingly, under his bed. Without taking his clothes off, he lay face down on the bed. Bobbie was exhausted. His legs felt like two stiff boards. Both feet were stinging like they were being burned.

Lottie Mae wasn't home that November evening, because she was around the corner on Hall Street in a narrow, row house, getting rid of an unwanted child. To the medically minded, she was aborting, unnaturally.

Lottie Mae had made a previous vow to herself, after the difficult stillborn birth of her second child. She had vowed, "Ain't gonna have no mo' kids!" She had really meant it and had kept her word by having two abortions. This was number three on the abortion parade. It was, of course, a home remedy type of operation: a wood, kitchen table, germ-covered operating tools and an old, mammy mystic healer as doctor. Somehow, Lottie Mae had survived the previous butcherings, and was not worried about the present attempt. Anyway, Joe Wilson was paying for it. She didn't have to worry about the cost.

Lottie Mae squinted at the bright light as she lay back on the table and spread her legs, giving Miss Ellen a "bird's eye" view of her unshaved delta. Miss Ellen picked up the long, steel, blunt probe and the small, steel mallet, then she turned towards Lottie Mae. Exposing her brown-stained teeth in a smile, she said, "Don't have t' splain 'bout these." She spit into a can on the floor, and wiped the dark dribble off her chin with her apron.

"Sho don't. Gettin' tired lookin' at 'em, too!"

"If my old head is right, makes number three," Miss Ellen said and pointed to the mass of kinky white hair on her head.

"Sho do. . . . Joe gave ya money?" asked Lottie Mae.

"Fifty dollars. Gonna give me the res' nex' week," Miss Ellen answered. She spit, wiped her chin and stuck another wad of chewing tobacco into her mouth.

"Sho glad he kept his promise. Ain't got no money this time."

"Take a slug an' brace yo'self," Miss Ellen said, handing her a bottle of a cheap, blended whiskey.

Lottie Mae took a long drink without coughing or wincing from the burn in her throat. She and whiskey were old friends.

Using a wood broom handle for a hand brace and closing her eyes, she set herself for the ordeal, without any pain reliever—just whiskey. The ordeal continued for twenty minutes. She felt every scrape, every poke, every mallet stroke. Lottie Mae could only lie on the table and moan her pain away, while Miss Ellen stuck the blunt probe inside her body, hunting for the unwanted fetus. Finally, after relentless scraping, poking and cursing, the uterus reluctantly aborted its human baggage. With a rushing surge of blood and broken matter, the sickly looking mess blurted out of Lottie Mae into a dirty, chipped, agate pan. Miss Ellen heaved a sigh of relief. She disposed of the murdered matter with a noisy flush of the toilet.

Lottie Mae spent the next day in bed on the pretense of sickness. The bleeding had stopped. But she was still weak from the night's loss of blood. She was waiting, anxiously. Miss Ellen had promised to visit and examine her. The previous abortions had somehow been successful, in spite of Miss Ellen's crude technique. But this was the

47

first time Lottie Mae felt feverish. She wanted to forget
it as only natural, and hoped the fever would go away
in a few days. But she couldn't forget the fever and felt
uneasy about it. Fear and fever made her feel chilly,
damp and hot at the same time. It seemed like Miss
Ellen would never come.

Finally, the extremely overweight Miss Ellen was
heard treading heavily up the stairway, bringing Lottie
Mae the medicine and hope needed for her recovery.
Lottie Mae had faith in her; more so than with any doctor
in the clinic. She liked her personal touch. The friendly
way she advised about life, medicine and love.

Miss Ellen pushed the doorway's soiled curtain aside,
and entered Lottie Mae's bedroom with the confidence
of a visiting medical doctor. She carried a bulky black
satchel. It contained love potions as well as medicines.
She had a secret love potion formula that was guaranteed
to work. It's origin was from some obscure bayou in the
Louisiana delta country; Miss Ellen being originally from
the Louisiana-Mississippi River area.

She stood over Lottie Mae with her great hulk of a
body and her mounds of clothing and stared silently.

Lottie Mae smiled weakly and motioned her to sit
down. Miss Ellen backed into the chair with effort. The
chair creaked and sagged under her bulk. She looked
like a whitecapped mountain bulging at its sides. The
black satchel fell heavily to the worn, pine wood floor.
Miss Ellen stared silently, for over a minute, before she
began the official visit. It was part of the packaged deal;
the post-abortion visit with an injection of solace.

"Look hot, honey. Feel hot?"

"Yes, mam. Got fever all over!" Lottie Mae replied,
drawing in her lower lip.

Miss Ellen put a wrinkled, brown-skinned hand on

Lottie Mae's damp forehead. "Sleep any las' night?" She stared at Lottie Mae with dull eyes.

"Not much."

"Look a little tired, honey," confided Miss Ellen. "Got some sleepin' potion. Leave it with ya, befo' I go."

"Thank ya kindly, Miss Ellen."

"Let's get on t' yo' trouble," Miss Ellen said. "Where's it hurtin' ya, honey?" She shifted the wad of tobacco in her mouth and waited for the reply.

"Up where the baby was."

"Feels like a fire's burnin' inside?"

"Yes, mam, like somebody stuck a hot poker up there!" Lottie Mae drew in her lower lip again.

Miss Ellen patted Lottie Mae on the arm in her best bedside manner. She consoled her in a soft voice, a touch of the familiar South in it. "Don't fret none, honey. Gonna stop all that fever an' hurtin'." She paused, expelled a sigh, then continued speaking. "Got some good pain killer an' fever reducer. Give it t' ya right now, while yo' boy is out." She spit into a handkerchief and shifted the wad inside her mouth.

While his mother was being treated by Miss Ellen, Bobbie was spending the day with the gang. He had his audience perched on the steps of the elementary school porch, listening to his story. Bobbie had them leaning forward with their mouths open, and their big unblinking eyes, staring at him. The final scene under the bridge with the bricks, made them laugh. It was just too much. The story finished, Bobbie gave his audience a chance to comment. He was enjoying the moment of glory and wanted to make the feeling linger as long as possible.

Junior McVeigh made the first comment. "Let's get back at 'em, Bobbie. Carter ain't got a lotta friends."

"Carter can wait. Get him any day after school."

Searching the faces, Bobbie sensed agreement with his opinion. Before anyone could comment, he continued, "Like I said befo', Carter ain't shit. His jive-ass friends ain't shit! Beat 'em anytime we feels like it!" Bobbie's eyes widened. He waited for their reactions.

The last statement brought the usual loud shouts of agreement. After they calmed down, Bobbie told them about his ideas for raising money.

He outlined his plans for the next few weeks. They would keep on breaking into cars, steal hub caps, pilfer glove compartments; plus remove complete wheels when possible and anything else that can be carried away. The first thing they would do would be to steal tools; bumper jacks and wrenches.

The gang agreed to the new petty crime policy and were eager to begin.

CHAPTER 7

Bobbie's return to school that following week was disappointing. He had expected to be called down to the principal's office or to the guidance counselor; maybe even to see the discipline officer. But since he didn't even get passing notice from anyone in authority, he felt they really didn't care about him or his problems. Even his teachers were rather cool towards him, accepting his return as routine. Bobbie resented the lack of interest.

He drifted through the few remaining school days in November without getting in trouble. Bobbie never really liked school—just tolerated it. With December and the approach of Christmas, he began thinking about the things he would like to have. The money from the small "jobs" wasn't enough. He wanted a lot more for the holidays. "Talk it over with the gang," he pondered, "maybe we could pull a job on a gas station." He thought about that for most of the day.

That night, outside the club, Bobbie gathered the others as they arrived for an evening's fun.

They walked down Main Street and sat on the worn, porch steps of an old, abandoned, cracker factory. It was more secluded for the conversation that was to follow.

Bobbie presided over the meeting, as usual, and opened the discussion with a question.

"Do ya wanna be broke this Christmas?" Not waiting for an answer, he continued; "Not gonna make much from hub caps. Ain't got but two tires so far. Was thinkin'. Let's go big. Break in a gas station." Then with an anxious,

51

almost pleading tone to his voice, he asked, "What do ya think?"

Calvin, the usually more cautious member, made the first comment. "If we get caught, be in lotsa trouble."

"Yeah, but only creeps get caught!" Bobbie replied.

Larry Johnson asked Bobbie, "If we get caught, where they send us? Prison on Fo'th Street?" The top of his beaked nose raised and lowered itself four times while he spoke.

Looking at the ground in front of him, an inflection of digust in his voice, hands on hips and legs apart, Bobbie asked, "What's all this stupid talk 'bout gettin' caught? If'n we wasn't smart, be caught long time 'go!"

Junior McVeigh's low, hoarse voice was heard from the rear of the group. "Man, what so hard 'bout breakin' in a gas station?"

This was the reaction that Bobbie was hoping to get from somebody in the gang. He answered in a confident tone, "Ain't nothin' hard 'bout it," continuing with the same breath, "ain't no gas station 'round here can't be broken in." Bobbie glanced at each one, then said, "All we got t' do is be on the ball an' have lookouts. Won't get caught by the cops. Have time t' get away an' hide!" His voice grew loud on the last word, almost squeaking.

"Y. . . Y. . . Ya got any place in mind, Bobbie," Jimmie asked.

Bobbie answered, "No, but I was hopin' we'd look 'round, maybe find an easy one fo' the first job." With a high pitched voice, he said, "Knows we can do it! Won't get caught!" Bobbie rotated his head, and looked at each one. Seeking their total agreement, he asked, almost whispering, "How many wants t' pull a job?"

Junior and Jimmie agreed without waiting and Larry agreed, after some prodding by Bobbie. Calvin took longer to convince; finally he agreed. Bobbie adjourned the meeting, after getting everyone's promise they would start "casing" all the neighborhood stations, and the ones on the way home from school. It had been a good meeting. He led them back to the club, feeling satisfied.

Within a week they had located and entered their first gas station. Their confidence raised considerably, they had a second gas station "zeroed in" with the date, time and method of entry figured out in advance. It was going to be the station at River Drive and Garment Street on Thursday, December 11 at 8:00 p.m., and they would enter through a rear window. Bobbie had made the final decision on Wednesday, the tenth.

Thursday night was ink black with a heavy layer of clouds bearing in steadily from the west. The wind was blowing in gusts off the river at ten to twenty miles per hour. It was cold, not severely cold, but cold enough to have the promise of snow in its twisting, invisible currents. The season's first snowstorm was in the making, and with it the promise of a white Christmas. While the city's populace was Christmas shopping in the brisk night air, with the gayly decorated streets announcing the yuletide season; five youths were gathering at the dark corner of Capital and Alliance Streets, across from a triangular-shaped playground. Because of the open playground area, the whipping winds seemed more severe. The chilled, night air pierced their lightweight jackets.

Calvin was last to arrive at the exposed corner, and was greeted impatiently by the cold, shivering group. Having told their parents they were going to the Youth Club, they wanted to get the "job" finished by nine that night.

With his breath a visible, gray vapor under the street light, Bobbie asked Calvin, "Where ya been? Should've started by now!"

"Aw, man, had t' go t' the sto'."

"Did ya bring the crowbar an' sack?"

"Yeah, got 'em, right here." Calvin showed them the bundle inside his coat.

"Got the screwdrivers, Larry?" asked Bobbie.

"Yeah. Brought a penknife too!" answered Larry, his nose twitching.

"Good. I got the flashlight. All we gotta do now is get inside," replied Bobbie. "Did good on las' week's job. Do this one same as las' week's."

"Aw, B . . . B . . . Bobbie, I was lookout las' week," interrupted Jimmie.

"Don't get excited, Jimmie! You'll get a chance. We's gonna do this one like las' week's." Pointing his left index finger at Calvin, he said, "We'll go inside." Looking at Jimmie with a half-smile, he said, "You'll wait outside an' han' the tools in. When we's done, we'll han' out the tools an' sack."

"O . . . O . . . Okay," Jimmie said, blinking his eyes rapidly and shifting his cold feet.

"Larry an' Junior, you'll be lookouts. Show ya where I wants ya t' stay," instructed Bobbie, who checked out every detail. He wanted this one to be done right. Bobbie motioned the direction with his head and said, "Let's go."

The gang walked across a silent Capital Street, then down an empty Alliance Street in complete silence. Calvin, Jimmie, Larry and Junior were quietly waiting for cues from Bobbie, who was walking in front of them, his body tilted forward against the wind.

On Garment Street, a hundred feet from the rear of the gas station, Bobbie suddenly stopped walking. The cue was immediately followed by the others. They stopped. No one talked. They just stared at Bobbie, waiting for orders. The orders came with surprising swiftness, considering the source. Standing on the concete curb under a maple tree's naked limbs, Bobbie had a good view of the station. From this field position, the little general gave his orders.

"Larry, stan' nex' t' the fence. See where I mean?" asked Bobbie, pointing towards the station.

Larry squinted and shivered, fixed his position, then answered, "Yeah."

"Junior, get on the other side nex' t' the fence."

Junior asked Bobbie, "River Drive side?"

"Yeah, an' watch both ways."

Larry said, "Be checkin' both ways on my side, too!"

Bobbie ordered, "Junior, go first. When he's 'cross, then you, Larry. Okay, get goin'."

Junior tried to walk calmly across the street, but somehow couldn't shake the uneasy feeling from his gait. He kept glancing to either side with a half-turning motion.

Larry followed Junior across, after he had disappeared between the high, wood fence and the cinder block building. Larry looked back, across the street at Bobbie, Calvin and Jimmie, before he stepped into the narrow alleyway.

Bobbie waited, allowing enough time for them to get into position. He turned towards Calvin and Jimmie and said, "Checked it out this afternoon. Got some cartons fulla empty oil cans on the side. Befo' we walk 'round the back, we grabs one. Use 'em t' stan' on. Winda's high."

Calvin asked Bobbie, "Think this crowbar's 'nough?"

"Yeah," Bobbie answered, nodding his head.

Jimmie said, "I . . . I . . . I . . . hopes I can reach. W . . . W . . . When ya needs the tools." He stared at Bobbie, blinking his eyes rapidly, mouth still open.

"Be high 'nough," Bobbie answered.

"Now?" asked Calvin.

"Yeah, let's go," answered Bobbie.

They stayed in the shadows, walking silently in single file. When they came abreast of the station, Bobbie made a final check of the street for traffic and people. He was

55

satisfied. It was empty; no people, no cars. Nodding his permission, they quickly crossed the street and disappeared into the darkness, between the station's rear wall and the parallel, six-feet high, wood fence.

In crouched and kneeling positions, they waited with their hands gripping the boxes. Bobbie took the expected lead and placed his box first against the unpainted cinder block wall. Calvin placed his on top of Bobbie's with Jimmie placing his uppermost.

Bobbie took out the flashlight, keeping it unlit, he used it to motion Calvin to climb up the cardboard pyramid. Calvin would work in the darkness. The flashlight would be used inside, only.

With the high, wooden fence concealing him, Calvin labored with the crowbar, trying to spring the window's catch. He tried to work the end of the crowbar between the stationary, metal framing and the movable sections of the window.

After tense, silent waiting, Bobbie whispered to Calvin, "How's it comin'?"

Calvin reported in a low voice, "Can't get my crowbar in right. Too tight! Might have t' break the glass."

Bobbie felt a sudden uneasy twinge, when he heard the last word, glass. Breaking the glass would be too risky! Too noisy! Somebody might hear them!

"Don't break the winda," Bobbie whispered.

"How we gonna get in?"

"Heck with it. Jes won't get in t'night," answered Bobbie, while he rubbed his cold hands and shuffled his cold feet for warmth, glad that it wasn't snowing. He looked up at the starless, black night. "Gonna snow yet," he said to himself.

After ten agonizing minutes, that were almost unbearable, Calvin announced in an excited whisper, "Made it! Catch's startin' t' give!"

Bobbie almost forgot himself, but managed to keep his voice low and whispered back, "That's good. Keep at it."

Bobbie felt tight inside, like a newly strung archery bow. He was sweating in spite of the cold. He thought to himself, "Can't stan' much mo' waitin'." Trying to ease the tense waiting, he kept whispering encouragement to Calvin.

Finally, after five long minutes, the catch snapped with a loud click. Bobbie and Jimmie both blew vaporous sighs. Calvin just stood still and rubbed his chin nervously, waiting for the next move.

Bobbie recovered quickly and started the operation moving. He told Calvin to pass down the crowbar and climb into the station. Handing everything to Jimmie, Bobbie mounted the window sill and received the tools, flashlight and sack from Jimmie.

Bobbie felt good. He was in his element and liked the excitement, despite its fatiguing strain on his nerves. He climbed carefully into the station and welcomed Calvin's helpful grip, making a successful landing on the station's concrete floor.

Calvin and Bobbie walked slowly, feeling their way carefully. They didn't want to use the flashlight too often. The only light came filtering in from the street lamp, keeping the station in a variety of eerie shadows.

"Let's check out the office first," Bobbie suggested. He led the way and shortly tripped over the steel lift. The sharp pain made him gasp. He sat down and stretched out the hurt leg.

"Ya okay?" asked Calvin.

"Bumped my leg. Better walk 'round me," answered Bobbie, rubbing his sore right leg, fighting back tears.

They walked the rest of the way without a mishap and stopped to check outside, through the glass doorway

57

and windows. With the office being the most exposed part of the station, they wanted to be extra careful.

In a crouched position, they duck-waddled to the desk. Calvin searched the drawers, while Bobbie looted the open cash register drawer of two dollars and eighty-five cents in change.

Calvin found a box of advertising pens in the top drawer. The others had only useless items. He stuffed the box of pens into the sack, and turned towards the shelves on the wall. He said to Bobbie, "Help me get this stuff."

"Hol' it open. I'll throw the stuff in."

The stuff consisted of boxed headlamps, tubes, hose clamps, car polish, motor cleaner, radiator cleaner, light bulbs, fuses and sundry items their greedy fingers failed to recognize, and much less cared, in the darkness.

"Better stop. Gettin' heavy," Calvin said. "Got plen'y."

"Yeah, let's get outta here," Bobbie agreed. He rubbed his head with his left hand and stared at the heavy sack.

Blinking the flashlight occasionally, they dragged the sack to the rear window. It was heavier than expected. The two of them had to drag it together. When they stopped under the window, both were puffing.

Calvin suggested, "Better take some out. Too heavy." He looked at the huge sack propped against the wall.

"Lighten it outside."

"Too heavy t' lif' through," answered Calvin. He looked up at the window, then at Bobbie.

"Take some heavy boxes out," Bobbie said.

The sack lightened, they lifted it through the window, resting it on the cinder block ledge. Bobbie called Jimmie. "Get Larry an' Junior. It's heavy."

Because he was helping Jimmie, Junior wasn't in position to see the police patrol car that came cruising slowly down River Drive, heading toward the center of town. The patrolman driving was too occupied with the controls to notice anything. But his companion thought he saw shadows moving inside the gas station. They decided to check out the station more carefully, turned right into Carter Street and another right turn on Garment Street. Stopping about a hundred feet from the station, they quietly exited from the car, drew their thirty-eight caliber pistols and advanced slowly toward the station. They paused at the edge of the fence, and peered cautiously around it into the dark alleyway. The policemen watched three, youthful shadows lower a large, bulky object to the ground. Shining their flashlights directly at the boys, they ordered in unison; "Don't move! Stay where you are!" The lights and the firm, adult voices froze the three youths into statues.

Junior, Jimmie and Larry were lined up with palms against the cinder block wall by the one officer, while the other mounted the makeshift platform and blasted the two faces inside with his flashlight. Bobbie and Calvin were stunned by the sudden light, and the officer's voice ordering them out. They climbed out of the window and lined up with the others.

All five boys were obeying the police officers' commands in stunned, scared silence. They could hardly believe what was happening to them. It didn't seem real.

With the sack as evidence, stuffed into the car's trunk and the five boys crammed into the rear seat, the entire package was delivered enmasse to the Second Precinct Police Station on South Enterprise Street. They were hustled inside and put into an empty room to await questioning. It was the room's blank, gray walls that brought all of them back. They woke up and looked at each other in troubled silence.

Jimmie broke the silence. "W . . . W . . . What'll they do with us, B . . . B . . . Bobbie?"

With his chin resting on his chest, Bobbie answered, "Don't much care." He lifted his head to look at Calvin. "Put too much in the sack. Got hoggy."

Calvin answered without taking his eyes off his shoes, "Yeah."

The others nodded in agreement, then returned to more silent staring at the floor, walls or anything else that seemed to need staring. Words seemed out of place, especially wisecracks. The staring contest was disrupted by police necessity: names and addresses had to be secured; next of kin and details about the aborted, illegal entry; the breakdown of the gang, who was the leader, who followed. They wanted to know all the details and more if possible.

Bobbie was the last one to be questioned. He walked into the interrogation room, trying to act like he didn't care. But inside, his heart was pounding. He felt warm and damp throughout his entire body.

"Sit down, boy," ordered Sergeant Frank Macky. His blue eyes studied Bobbie in detail. He rubbed a sore on his cheek and scanned the sheet of paper on the desk.

Bobbie sat down without answering. He fought back the tears and almost choked, forcing the lump in his throat to go down.

"Your friends said you're the leader. Told me you planned the whole thing." A skeptical smile parted his thick lips. "True?" Sergeant Macky stared at Bobby. His acne-covered face appeared even redder from the light overhead.

Bobbie wondered, "Did the others talk?" He didn't answer the sergeant's question, but kept thinking to himself, "What's the use. Find out anyways." Then he answered with a steady voice, "Yeah, I'm the leader. I planned the job.

"Almost got away with it," Sergeant Macky replied. "But, you didn't! Hope this taught you a lesson!"

Bobbie stayed quietly withdrawn, and refused to grant any sign that he heard the sergeant. He just stared at the sergeant's reddish, puffy skin, his crooked nose, and his large ears. The largest ears Bobbie had ever seen. They were as red as the sergeant's face.

"What's your full name, boy?"

"Bobbie Lee."

"Robert Lee?"

"No, Bobbie Lee."

"All right, what's your address?"

"120 Alliance Street. 'partment on the third flo'."

"Age?"

"Fo'teen."

"Mother's name?"

"Lottie Mae Lee."

"She lives with you?"

"Yeah."

"You got a father?"

"Lives down South," Bobbie answered, feeling warm again. He answered the rest of the routine questions about school, relatives and explained about his mother's caseworker and their relief situation.

"That's all I need for now. Go downstairs and wait with the others. We're taking you to the County Youth House." Sergeant Macky located the sore on his cheek again and squeezed. The yellowish puss blurted out on his fingers. He watched Bobbie leave and wiped his fingers on a handkerchief.

CHAPTER 8

The journey to the County Youth House was ironical. Leaving the Second Precinct Station in two, police sedans, they motored down Carter Street, past the state prison and into River Drive, a short distance from the gas station.

In the rear of each car the silence became rigidly awkward. Without exception, eyeballs floated in salty tears, throats were lumpy and stomachs harbored nervous, fluttering butterflies. They stared mutely through the windows, seeing little of the city's buildings, lights or the naked, crooked-limbed sycamore trees along River Drive. Starless, the night made the river appear dark, brooding and ominous, blending with their moods.

A right turn off River Drive onto Park Avenue put them into a strange part of the city: a sprawling school, reflecting a vague, shadowy outline; towering tree trunks, dimly visible in the dark, rambling interior of Washington Park and three-story mansions squatting grandly at the top of the terraced, manicured lawns, almost beyond their view. This scenic parade flicked rapidly past them; of little interest to the five sad youths.

Bobbie and company were jostled rudely out of their sullen, indifferent moods, when the cars screeched to a halt, facing a long, one story, beige-colored brick building of modern design.

They were processed quickly and placed in individual cells for the remainder of the night.

Bobbie lay awake on his bunk, staring vaguely at the strange cell with its white, ceramic tile walls, the unusual toilet that could only be flushed by the office and the door with its handle and hinges on the outside. It was a room without knobs or handles to pull or break; a modern cell designed from experience with disturbed, angry youths.

He closed his eyes. The night's events flashed across his memory screen. He recalled vividly the blinding, painful light blasting against his face, the search facing the wall, the police interview, word for word, in the small, undecorated room on the second floor. Bobbie relived the sad, quiet ride through the city's dark, shadowy streets and the abrupt halt, causing him to bump his head against the front seat. He felt the painful lump on his forehead, almost forgotten by the strange surroundings. Bobbie thought about the new, brick, modern building with its low profile and glass doors, the friendly night attendant who processed them, the long hallway with its many doors, gradually reducing the size of their marching group down to him, standing in front of a green metal door.

His eyes felt warm and wet, overflowing into tiny streams down the sides of his face, past his temples and ears, dripping onto the bed. The sobs echoed off the tile walls. Realizing their source, Bobbie wiped his face with the wool blanket. He said to himself, "Bet they cried, too." Feeling embarrassed, but glad no one saw or heard him cry, he shrugged it off and turned over on his left side. Bobbie squeezed his eyes shut, anxiously seeking sleep.

Breakfast was a new experience for the group. They were the main attraction; stared at and talked about by the other youths. The introductions were informal and the reasons for being there were discreetly overlooked by the staff. Not until they were in the enclosed, asphalt-

63

paved courtyard during the outdoor game period, did the group get a chance to talk.

Huddled around Bobbie, they anxiously fired questions at him, seeking security in his leadership. Calvin asked Bobbie, "How long they keep ya here?"

Bobbie thought about it, then answered, "Guess 'til our trial comes up."

"Trial!" Larry said. The tip of his nose twitched up and down.

"Not so loud!" Calvin said. "Want ev'rybody t' hear?"

Keeping himself under control, Larry tried again, "Thought they has trials fo' big people; not fo' no kids." His nose twitched again.

Bobbie answered, "Talked t' that big, skinny kid, ya know, the one that sat nex' t' me." Bobbie waited for them to nod, confirming their memories, then continued, "He said they keep ya here, 'til yo' trial comes up. Has the trial right here!"

"W . . . W . . . What kinda trial? L . . . L . . . Like the ones on television?" asked Jimmie. He blinked his eyes at Bobbie.

"Don't think so. The skinny kid, . . . can't remember his name, . . . said they has a judge an' the cops what caught ya."

"H . . . H . . . How 'bout yo' folks?" Jimmie asked. "D . . . D . . . Does they come?" His mouth left open, after the last question, he blinked his eyes again.

"Didn't say nothin' 'bout folks. Guess they comes, too!"

Junior McVeigh commented, "Bet are folks was surprised."

Calvin replied, "Mus' been really surprised! Mad, too! My daddy's pickin' out a big stick right now, fo' tannin' my hide!" ·

That was enough to bring smiles and quiet laughter

to the group, helping them feel more at ease. Calvin laughed the loudest.

While Bobbie and his gang were talking in the courtyard, the Youth House Director, John Higgins, was reviewing the police report of their arrest. He was a word reader and progressed slowly, moving his lips with each word. Finishing, he flicked on the intercom and ordered the day attendant to bring Bobbie Lee to his office. John Higgins hated to waste time. While waiting for Bobbie's arrival, he picked up the telephone and dialed the county welfare office. He asked for Miss Kelly but she wasn't available, so he left a message to have her call him. John Higgins had just returned the receiver, when Bobbie entered his office. Bobbie sat down, avoiding recognition by Mr. Higgins. With his large black eyes, he stared intently at the brown asphalt tile floor.

John Higgins observed Bobbie's entrance, his obvious attitude and his present silence. He decided to outwait his young adversary, so both of them just sat there; Bobbie staring at the floor, Mr. Higgins staring at him. After five, silent, awkward minutes, he decided to change his tactics. John Higgins cleared his throat adjusted his eyeglasses and asked, "You're Bobbie Lee, aren't you?" He thought he heard an answer, leaned forward, and asked, "What did you say?" John Higgins' pale white skin wrinkled around his pale, gray-blue eyes.

"Yeah, I'm Bobbie Lee," Bobbie mumbled.

"You mean, yes, Mr. Higgins. Now let me hear that answer again, Bobbie." John Higgins pushed his sliding eyeglasses back to the narrow bridge of a long, narrow nose with teardrop-shaped nostrils.

After a pause. . . . "Yes, Mr. Higgins," Bobbie said without looking up.

Winning round one, Mr. Higgins smiled, revealed a

65

mouth full of false teeth and decided to move forward from his established beachhead. He cleared his throat and said, "I've been reading the police report. It names you as the leader. Anything to say about that?"

"Nothin' . . . Mr. Higgins."

"How did you get to be leader?"

"Jes leads, that's all!" After a pause, "Mr. Higgins."

Not one to give up easily, John Higgins switched his approach again. "Live alone with your mother?"

"Yes."

"Does she work?"

"No."

"How does she support you?"

"We's on relief," Bobbie answered, feeling uneasy from the question.

"Then you must have a caseworker."

"Miss Kelly."

"Does she visit often?"

"Ev'ry couple months."

"Do you like the social worker?"

Resisting an impulse to tell about his dislike for Miss Kelly, Bobbie replied, "Guess she's all right."

"What do you mean by that answer?" Mr. Higgins coughed into his closed right fist, cleared his throat and waited for a reply. His pale, gray-blue eyes fixed on Bobbie.

"Guess she could be worse."

"What you mean is that you don't like her, . . . isn't that so?"

"Yeah . . . guess so."

Winning round two, Mr. Higgins again switched his interviewing attack. "Does your mother belong to a church?"

"No."

"Do you go to Sunday school?"

"No."

John Higgins concluded to himself, "This kid's a tough one to get to. No use wasting anymore of my time today." He adjusted his brown, horn-rimmed eyeglasses and said, "We've talked enough today. We'll get together again soon. If you have any questions, feel free to see me."

Bobbie decided to take advantage of the present interview, "Got a question now, Mr. Higgins." Not waiting for permission, he asked, "How long we gonna be here, befo' are trial comes up?"

"Well," Mr. Higgins said. He cleared his throat before continuing, "Won't be held until the holidays are over. Should be sometime in January—next year."

"One mo' question, Mr. Higgins. Is parents allowed t' come?"

"Yes they're requested to be present," Mr. Higgins answered and decided, "he can talk when he wants to."

"Thank you, Mr. Higgins. Can I go now?"

"Yes," replied Mr. Higgins, realizing he had lost round three. Observing Bobbie's confident departure, he was aware of having been outsmarted by the youth. He didn't quite know how it happened. "He's no dummy," John Higgins said to himself, watching Bobbie leave. He hated to lose control of anything, especially to adolescents. His eyeglasses didn't need adjusting, but he adjusted them anyway.

An hour later, Miss Kelly returned Mr. Higgins' telephone call. He picked the telephone up after the second ring. John Higgins never answered a telephone until it rang twice. He identified himself. Martha Kelly was excited, didn't waste any time with pleasantries: "Mr. Higgins, Miss Kelly."

"Oh . . . yes, Miss Kelly, how are you?"

"Bobbie Lee's mother was rushed to the hospital last night. They don't expect her to live much longer." A long silence made her ask, "Are you still there?"

"Yes, I'm still here," he answered. "It's just the sudden statement. I wasn't prepared for it."

"I've never been one to beat around the bush." Martha Kelly brushed an untidy wisp of red hair away from her eyes.

"Has she been sick?"

"No, she had an abortion. Complications have set in. The doctor told me she's hemorrhaging again, and she's got blood poisoning from an internal infection."

"Who took her to the hospital?"

"The police did. When they went to the apartment to report her son's arrest, they found her unconscious in bed."

"Oh! Poor woman." John Higgins pushed his sliding eyeglasses back with his right thumb.

"Don't feel sorry for her. She's put herself into this predicament. Tried to straighten her out, but she was one of those know-it-all people."

"But, even so, can't help feeling sorry for her." John Higgins coughed into his right hand.

"Feel more sorry for the boy," confided Miss Kelly. "How are we going to break the news to him?"

After ten seconds, John Higgins answered, "I'll do it, tonight, when he's alone. Won't say anything about her poor condition; just that she's sick and in the hospital."

"Yes, that should be enough for now. I'll be in contact with the hospital. I'll call, if anything further develops."

"Thank you for the call, Miss Kelly, good-bye."

"Good-bye, Mr. Higgins."

With his hand still resting on the telephone, John Higgins stared at it as if he didn't believe what it had just told him. He returned to action and buzzed the day attendant. "Charlie, I'll be back after supper. Have to see one of the new boys, Bobbie Lee. Don't say anything to anyone. His mother's in bad shape at City Hospital. Don't expect her to pull through. Tell the night attendant to expect me around nine."

Promptly at 9:00 p.m., John Higgins entered the building, announced his presence to the night attendant and walked down the empty, silent corridor. He stopped in front of a green door with the yellow numeral nine. John Higgins was nervous and had a dry, pinchy throat that felt like sandpaper every time he swallowed. Putting his right hand to his neck, he commented to himself, "Hope I'm not getting another cold." After finding the correct key, he adjusted his eyeglasses and cleared his throat, before opening the door.

Bobbie was still lying awake in bed. The sudden light and the door opening were startling. He was completely confused, when Mr. Higgins entered his cell. All Bobbie could utter in the way of a greeting was, "Mr. Higgins!" He sat up quickly.

John Higgins didn't quite know how to begin. Nervously, he ran his right hand over his thinning gray hair, rubbed his thin right leg and knobby right knee, then adjusted his eyeglasses which didn't need adjusting.

Coughing and then clearing his throat, he said, "I know you're surprised to see me, Bobbie but I wanted to see you alone, without calling you to my office. I know you'll be expecting your mother to visit Sunday. I wanted to see you about her."

Bobbie stiffened. He asked, "Somethin' wrong? Can't come an' see me?"

"Yes. She won't be able to come Sunday." John Higgins rubbed his knee again.

Bobbie remained silent, leaning on his elbows. He

stared past Mr. Higgins, wondering what could be wrong with his mother.

Bobbie heard Mr. Higgins speak, the words seemed to come from a distant sound chamber; "Your mother isn't feeling well. She had to be taken to the hospital."

"She what?"

"Didn't you hear me, Bobbie? I said she had to be taken to the hospital. She isn't feeling well!"

"The hospital?"

"Yes, the hospital!" John Higgins' eyes became larger and his eyeglasses slid down his nose.

Realizing the seriousness of the answer, Bobbie asked, "She hurt?"

"I don't know, Bobbie," answered Mr. Higgins. "All I know is that she isn't feeling well, and had to be taken there."

"Will I get a chance t' see her?"

"I don't know, but if it can be arranged, you'll get to see her," Mr. Higgins said without too much confidence. He stood up, signaling the end of the conversation. "I'll be getting more information tomorrow about your mother's condition. Don't worry, everything is going to be alright. . . . Good night, Bobbie."

"Good night, . . . Mr. Higgins," Bobbie answered, mouthing the words as if he weren't really certain he was speaking. Already the thought flashed across his brain: "Joe Wilson hurt her bad."

Five minutes after Mr. Higgins closed the door, the light blinked out and the room became silent and dark. For the next hour, Bobbie lay awake staring at the darkness. Mr. Higgins' vapid advice couldn't prevent anxious thoughts about his mother. Finally, a flood of tears brought relief. Exhausted, he fell asleep.

CHAPTER 9

Lottie Mae died quietly in an eight-bed ward at City Hospital, without religious absolution, attending relatives or friends. She gasped twice for breath, choked on the air and fell silent. It was over in seconds. Her death was detected by the floor nurse on a routine bed check and verified by the resident intern. Lottie Mae's body was promptly removed to the hospital morgue to await an autopsy, and Martha Kelly of the County Welfare Department was notified of her death.

Martha Kelly squeezed her county-owned Ford sedan into a parking space designed for a Volkswagen, and had to wiggle herself out of the half-opened door. After stepping out sideways and suffering only minor damage, she muttered to herself; "Never get a decent parking place! City-owned and can't even afford a bigger parking yard."

Martha Kelly stopped at the glass, double door entrance, straightened her brown cloth coat and rubbed the mud marks away. Despite her efforts, she made her usual rumpled appearance at the hospital; wisps of graying hair among the red stuck out from underneath the hood attached to her coat. With long, masculine strides, she walked from doorway to information desk and waited impatiently for service. Five minutes elapsed, before she was approached by the receptionist.

"May I help you?" asked an elderly woman.

"Yes, you may," snapped Martha Kelly. "I'd like to

know the status of a clinic patient admitted Thursday night. Her name's, Lottie Mae Lee."

"One moment, I'll check."

After five minutes of checking, the receptionist reported, "She died this morning at 2:00 a.m. Her body's in the morgue for an autopsy."

"Who ordered it?"

"Coroner."

"Can I see the doctor, who pronounced her dead?"

"If he's available; I'll need your name and relationship."

"I'm Martha Kelly. County Welfare Department. I was the deceased's caseworker."

"It may take awhile, Miss Kelly. You may wait in the reception lounge."

"All right, I'll wait."

Martha Kelly hated hospitals; their antiseptic odors and the people who staffed them. She hated waiting for doctors. When she wanted to see someone, it meant now, not an hour later. She hated those long hours during clinic visits with her clients.

To her surprise, in only a few minutes, an attractive young intern was standing over her. Jeffrey Roth was twenty-seven but looked more like twenty: a bright, even smile, black hair cut close in crew cut style, dark brown eyes and a clear olive complexion. He was six-one, not an ounce of fat, with the right amount of muscle, an impressive sight dressed in a white tunic.

"Miss Kelly, I'm Doctor Roth. May I help you?"

Martha Kelly was completely disarmed by the soft-spoken, good-looking intern. "Yes, Doctor Roth. I was the caseworker for Lottie Mae Lee. The woman you pronounced dead this morning."

"I see."

"Since Miss Lee was county supported, the funeral expense will have to be assumed by our department. When do you think the autopsy'll be finished?"

With his hands folded across his chest, he stared at the black and white, speckled terrazzo floor. After a few seconds, he said, "Probably not until Monday. That should give you enough time."

"Would you call me, after it's completed?"

"Yes."

She handed him her business card and ended the conversation. "Thank you. I'll be expecting your call."

"Good-bye, Miss Kelly. It was nice meeting you."

"Good-bye, Dr. Roth."

After Dr. Roth left, Martha Kelly hurried out of the hospital, away from the depressing building and its morbid atmosphere. She exhaled the antiseptic odor from her nostrils, squeezed back into her car, started the motor and drove out of the parking yard, tires squealing.

The first thing Martha Kelly did when she got back to her office, was to telephone the Youth House.

At the Youth House the telephone rang ominously. John Higgins hated the endless ringing. Finally, after the third annoying clang, he picked up the receiver with a slow deliberate motion and announced, "County Youth House, Mr. Higgins speaking."

An almost masculine voice responded from the other end. "Mr. Higgins, Miss Kelly. She's dead. Died early this morning."

"Anyone at her bedside."

"No. Went out of this lousy world, the way she came in—alone."

Not caring for the last descriptive remark, John Higgins changed the subject and asked, "When's the funeral?"

73

"After the autopsy."

"That'll give me time to soften the blow."

"Yes, it will."

"Let me know when and where. The boy should see his mother."

"Yes, I'll do that." Squinting at the clock on the wall, and anxious to end the depressing conversation, she replied, "I won't keep you any longer, Mr. Higgins, good-bye."

"Good-bye, Miss Kelly," John Higgins voiced without feeling, also relieved to end the conversation. He pushed his eyeglasses back with his right thumb and glanced at the small desk clock. It was lunchtime. But he didn't feel like eating.

Jimmie Heywood was behind Calvin in the cafeteria line with Larry and Junior behind him. They had been discussing Bobbie's peculiar behavior, during the morning play period in the courtyard and continued to talk about it, while waiting to be served.

"Y . . . Y . . . Yeah, man, h . . . h . . . he's been awful quiet all day!" exclaimed Jimmie He looked up at Calvin, blinked three times, then stared with wide black eyes, waiting for a reply

"Didn't say nothin', when I asked him 'bout his talkin' t' Mr. Higgins," Calvin complained to the others.

"His eyes been lookin' faraway, like he ain't even payin' attention," Larry added to the conversation, and the others nodded in agreement.

Junior McVeigh had noticed Bobbie leaving the court-yard during the play period and added his conclusion, "Saw Bobbie leave the yard durin' play period. Bet he was goin' t' Mr. Higgins' office."

Calvin, Jimmie and Larry nodded their heads at Junior, their faces serious. All four sat together and ate silently;

each in his own thoughts about Bobbie's strange, moody behavior.

When Bobbie was called to Mr. Higgins' office, he kept wondering about his mother's sudden sickness. "Wasn't sick Wednesday. Thursday, she's in a hospital. Somethin' strange goin' on."

Bobbie almost bumped into the door, then realizing whose door, knocked softly. He heard the "Come in" and opened the heavy, solid-oak door. Bobbie walked in, nodded to Mr. Higgins, mumbled a "Good morning" and sat down.

Mr. Higgins was on the telephone with Youth House business. He finished presently and put the receiver down. While observing Bobbie, he was aware of a strange feeling. John Higgins suddenly realized he disliked the position he was in and felt uncomfortable. He looked at Bobbie and frowned.

John Higgins decided to bypass all pleasantries, so difficult with Bobbie. "Was talking to Miss Kelly again. Your mother's very sick. A lot sicker, then when we talked yesterday." He stopped speaking, coughed and waited for the effect of his words but didn't see any facial or physical movement, only droplets of tears gathering in the corners of both eyes. He had thought, reporting she was very sick, would be better than immediately telling of her death. John Higgins looked at Bobbie's sad expression, and watched him fight back tears. He wondered about his decision to ease the impact of her death. John Higgins heard himself say, "I asked about taking you to see your mother, but Miss Kelly said she was too sick." Not getting any kind of reaction, he continued, "All we can do now is hope for the best." He took his eyeglasses off, wiped them clean, rubbed the two red marks on his nose and returned the eyeglasses.

75

Bobbie gulped noisily. Then the tears started pouring down both cheeks, looking like two faucet streams. He just sat there, not bothering to wipe them away and let them drip off his face, creating two circular damp spots on his shirt.

Mr. Higgins coughed, stood up and announced, "You can stay here, 'til you feel better. I've got to leave." Walking briskly by Bobbie, he patted him on the shoulder and stepped out of the room with noticeable relief.

The room's warm temperature had dried his tears but Bobbie remained in the chair. He was thinking—thinking about Joe Wilson. "Mus' been him. Mus' hurt my momma bad . . . t' get put in a hospital."

Bobbie hated Joe Wilson. He knew the feeling was mutual. Bobbie could never understand how his mother could stay with a man like him.

He remembered one particular Saturday last year, when he walked in the kitchen and saw his mother throw a dish at Joe Wilson. Bobbie recalled the drunken laugh, the awkward lunge, the brutal, relentless slaps, the punches and his mother's helpless screams. Bobbie remembered pounding his weak fists on that broad, hard back. He rubbed his chin, still feeling the adult slaps on his adolescent chin.

Bobbie remembered returning to the apartment in the afternoon and seeing the shocking scene. . . His mother drinking beer out of a can, laughing and enjoying herself with the same man who beat her that morning. Bobbie saw their faces in detail; Joe Wilson's mouth in a wide big-toothed smile with a dark husky arm around his mother. Her face marked from the beating. She was laughing from Joe Wilson's humorous comment. The scene made him wince. He felt uneasy, knowing he hated his mother a little that day, but he quickly pushed that feeling out of his mind.

Bobbie recalled walking through the hallway to his room, practically unnoticed by the two in the kitchen. He sat down on his bed and listened to their conversation. Their voices echoed through the thin wall.

"Now that we's straightened out, baby, gonna give me a little t'night?" Joe Wilson asked with drunken, slurred speech.

"Stop beatin' on me. Start treatin' me right."

"Ya knows how mad I gets, baby." Joe Wilson sucked at his beer can. A trickle of the amber-colored beer dripped off his chin, splashing on the table.

They both sipped from their beer cans and laughed. Lottie Mae felt his hand sliding inside her housecoat. The touch of his rough hand on her soft flesh sent sensual chills rippling across her body like waves disturbing a pond's still surface. She enjoyed the feeling but remembered Bobbie was in the apartment. She whispered, "Stop! Bobbie's home!"

"I know, baby. Can't help myself. Ya knows how much I loves ya," he cooed with a broad, heavy-lipped smile.

While Bobbie sat in Mister Higgins' office remembering the past scenes, his face contracted into a pained grimace. Erasing the images from his memory, he jumped off the chair and raced out of the office, away from the image of his mother and her lover.

Bobbie was the last one to eat and being alone was refreshing. The simple act of eating was enough activity to keep him from thinking about Joe Wilson and his mother. He could forget for the moment about them and himself.

When Sunday came, the day passed easily for everyone except Bobbie. He tried to act friendly with the other parents, but really wanted to be alone with his thoughts. Bobbie missed his mother and was worried. He couldn't understand her strange, sudden sickness.

After the parents left, Calvin and the others approached Bobbie, who was sitting in a leather chair glancing through a sports magazine. He appeared almost dwarfed by the large, green, lounging chair. Calvin was the first to speak. "My momma tol' me, yo' momma was taken t' the hospital."

"Y . . . Y . . . Yeah, same night we got c . . . caught," interrupted Jimmie.

"Yeah, I knows. Mr. Higgins tol' me all 'bout it."

"She feelin' bad?" asked Larry. His nose moving up and down, while he spoke.

"She sho is."

"Think they'll let ya go see her?" asked Calvin.

"Mr. Higgins said she's too sick. Hospital won't let nobody see her."

"What kinda hospital's that? Won't let nobody see their folks?" Junior asked everybody.

"Sounds no good t' me," Calvin answered for everybody, while they stared at Bobbie with sad faces. They stood awkwardly silent, unable to begin another subject; everything else seemed out of place. Bobbie refused to help. He remained silent and stared back at them.

CHAPTER 10

The basement autopsy room was windowless with pale green walls, gray cement floor and exposed piping overhead. A black rubber hose hung from the ceiling, dripping water into the gutter circling the slanted table. Stretched out on its corrugated white porcelain top was Lottie Mae Lee's body.

With one long scalpel stroke, the pathologist, dressed in a white, knee-length smock and brown rubber gloves, severed the body from chest to stomach. Then he pushed the inch thick layer of yellow fat and skin aside. Using sheers, he snipped and crunched each rib at an inverted angle in a "V" pattern from the stomach upward, toward each shoulder. He removed the severed rib cage in one section, placing it on the table next to him.

The body was now ready for entry. He lifted out the miles of multicolored intestines, plopping them next to the body with its legs and hands tied. As he removed each organ, he sliced it with a long, narrow, razor sharp knife, looking for signs of infection and disease. He took tissue samples of each organ and blood smears for laboratory tests to confirm the suspected cause of Lottie Mae's death—blood poisoning.

With the autopsy completed, he dumped the intestines into the body along with the liver, kidneys, spleen, lungs and heart. He replaced the rib cage and stitched the skin at three-inch intervals with a long, thick, sewing needle and rough cord. Then he placed the body on a stretcher and cóvered it with a manila-colored, water-resistant, paper sheet and pushed it through a wide metal doorway to its cubicle in the adjoining hospital morgue.

Jeffrey Roth notified Martha Kelly of the completed autopsy. She in turn notified John Higgins, who had the unpleasant job of telling Bobbie about his mother's death.

It was a chore but John Higgins told Bobbie about his mother that same day. Three days later, Bobbie and he drove to the funeral parlor to view Lottie Mae's body. Inside the car, the heater belched hot air. Bobbie unbuttoned his overcoat and suit jacket, peered through the vapor-smeared window at the minute flakes flicking past and commented, "Startin' t' snow."

"Yes, it is," John Higgins said. He glanced at Bobbie and noticed his unbuttoned clothing. "Feel warm? I'll shut off the heater."

They became silent again. They had been silent most of the way, with an occasional attempt at forced conversation. John Higgins had tried to discuss Bobbie's mother, but couldn't make any headway. He was lost for a beginning. Bobbie was sitting quietly trying to keep calm, fighting a nervous feeling in his stomach.

"Rides smooth, doesn't it, Bobbie?" asked John Higgins as he made a sharp left turn. This was his first new car and he was elated, despite their destination.

"Yeah."

It had that new car smell, look and touch. John Higgins looked at the shiny new dashboard and lighted instrument panel with secret pride, avoiding any revealing head movement. After a few minutes, he made another attempt to broach the subject. "I'm glad you decided to see your mother." Staring straight ahead, past the busy windshield wipers, he continued, "It was the right decision to make."

Bobbie had declined an earlier invitation to be taken

to the private funeral viewing, bursting into tears when told of his mother's death.

John Higgins had wisely allowed him to vent his emotions completely, before approaching the subject again. By suppertime, Bobbie had reversed his decision and decided to see his mother.

"I'm not 'fraid t' see my momma. I can take it."

John Higgins patted him on the shoulder, smiled and said, "I'm glad you changed your mind."

The small, but friendly gesture raised Bobbie's morale. He said to himself, "Mr. Higgins ain't a bad guy," while he dressed for the somber trip.

John Higgins parked the car in the newly paved parking yard behind the funeral home. The intense cold hurried their steps towards the one story, modernistic building of brick, stone and glass. The parking lot flood lights enhanced the beautiful pink marble and the long, thin, white Roman bricks. Landscaped with small, round, evergreen shrubs, the building was an impressive sight.

They stopped before a wide double doorway. The dark, solid-mahogany door was opened by a neatly dressed attendant with the right mood; subdued, discreet and courteous. They were ushered into a long, richly carpeted room. As they walked past the rows of empty metal chairs they could see the open casket and its contents.

At the sight of his mother, Bobbie shivered. He had never seen a corpse before. Looking up at Mr. Higgins, he said, "She looks different!"

John Higgins didn't reply but stood next to Bobbie, staring down at the dead woman with his right hand on Bobbie's left shoulder.

After five minutes of silent viewing, Bobbie became uneasy; not knowing what to say or how long to remain. He decided to wait for the cue from Mr. Higgins.

When a properly respectful interval had been counted by John Higgins' mental timekeeper, he looked down at Bobbie and said, "We can go now, Bobbie."

They walked quickly down the center aisle, a little too quickly. The room's quiet, morbid atmosphere had become too much for them. Even the flowers had a sweet, sickening odor.

The trip back to the Youth House allowed enough time for Bobbie to absorb the experience. When the car stopped in front of the steps, Bobbie realized he would never see his mother again and it struck him like a slap on the back of the head. He mumbled a quick good-bye to Mr. Higgins, and jumped out of the car. Bobbie couldn't walk fast enough down the empty, echoing corridor. Inside his room, he flung off his clothes, letting the pile build around him on the floor. Then Bobbie threw himself into the bed, pulling the sheet and blanket up to his neck. He held the pillow tightly around his head and sobbed face down into the white, clean bedsheet until he fell asleep.

The Youth House staff helped the season's holidays pass as cheerfully as possible in their unusual situation. Red and green crepe paper decorations, Christmas drawing and cutouts were made by the children. And they helped decorate the Christmas tree. Everyone received a Christmas present, along with the soda, cookies and cake at the Christmas party, and everyone was urged to be a part of the games and carol singing.

John Higgins and his staff, though they encouraged everyone to get into the spirit of Chrismas, were extra tactful with Bobbie, but did try to get him to join in the fun. It was pitiful to see him trying to be a part of it. He went through the motions but his thoughts were elsewhere. The staff members and children were aware of his feelings and didn't become obnoxious with their prodding or coaxing.

After the holidays, the Youth House returned to a normal routine. Bobbie came gradually out of his shell, and again became an active part of the Youth House program. Though they were kept active with arts and crafts and physical training periods, Bobbie and the other members of the gang were becoming anxious about their approaching trial. Since it was to be a new experience for them, they were preoccupied with their fears. It was apparent in their conversations.

It was arts and crafts period, and Jimmie was sanding one of his bookends. He had been thinking about the coming trial and was scared, because he thought they would have to go through one of those court trials similar to those seen on television and in the movies. With a creased brow and a concerned tone in his voice, Jimmie lifted his head, looked at Bobbie's profile and asked, "W . . . W . . . When do ya think th . . . the . . . they'll hol' the trial, B . . . Bobbie?" He blinked his eyes at Bobbie.

"Soon, I guess."

"Man, I'm . . . I'm gettin' tired of w . . . w . . . waitin'!" Jimmie confessed, with a higher pitch to his voice, almost squeaking.

"Me, too!" Bobbie agreed. "Gettin' tired stayin' here."

"D . . . D . . . Do ya think they'll t . . . take us away?" Jimmie asked; a worried look on his face. His eyes closed, he continued without waiting for the answer to his question. "If . . . If . . . they do, I . . . I . . hope I can take it."

Without looking at Jimmie, Bobbie answered with a firm voice, "If we goes, got t' take it!" Bobbie picked his head up and stared at Jimmie. "Don't want nobody cryin'. Look like we's nothin' but scared punks!"

"Y . . . Y . . . Yeah, that's right, Bobbie. W . . . W . . .

We got t' be tough," Jimmie agreed, staring straight ahead, trying to keep Bobbie from seeing his face. Silently, he returned to his unfinished bookend, and started sanding it vigorously—a little too vigorously. Bobbie watched Jimmie's right hand moving rapidly back and forth across the square piece of pine wood, but remained silent.

CHAPTER 11

Juvenile court trials in Hunts County are more informal than regular criminal or civil court proceedings; minus such judicial frills as a jury, prosecuting or defending attorneys. Justice is dispensed by the presiding judge only. The charge is presented by the arresting officer and reports are submitted by the state or county welfare departments or county probation office; whichever agency is involved with the offending juvenile. The judge reviews statements, reports, evidence and administers the sentence. His decision is final, without opportunity of appeal to a higher court. The sentence is usually confinement in a reformatory, placement under supervision of the county probation office or commitment to the state commission of child welfare. A sentence can be suspended and the youth placed with relatives under their responsibility and supervision. The court's sessions are usually held in the County Youth House with parents, other responsible relatives and interested professional people in attendance.

Juvenile Court was in session at the Youth House that third Wednesday in January. And it was a mild winter day. Mercerton was experiencing the January thaw: a few days during winter, when the temperature rises into the sixties, melting snow and thawing frozen ground.

The sun was shining brightly at a forty-five degree angle, and the brown drapes were drawn against its oblique rays. Despite the heavily lined drapes, it was warm in the rectangular-shaped room filled to capacity with people dressed for winter, suffering from an efficient heating system. The warm room and heavy winter clothing made it an uncomfortable waiting period.

The trial would begin promptly at 10:30 a.m. with Judge Henry Betts presiding, a punctual man who was proud of his judicial record. He never missed a day of court or never started sessions late. The overheated, sweating parents could depend on him to start the session promptly and complete it with minimum effort and time.

Judge Betts sat at the end of the long, shiny, walnut table. He was dressed in his favorite charcoal gray business suit, and was a young looking forty-eight with only a few specks of gray hair on each temple, blending with his auburn hair and ruddy complexion. The judge was in his usual stern, serious mood, his sharply pointed nose, cold brown eyes and rigid, angular jaw accented his feelings. His was a personal campaign against juvenile lawbreakers; especially their parents. Occasionally, he looked up from the reports, directing an extended, piercing stare at the five Negro boys until each one lowered his head, self-consciously. He liked to set a somber mood at his sessions.

The five boys were on Judge Betts' left, with Bobbie in the middle, Calvin and Larry on Bobbie's left and Jimmie and Junior nearest to the Judge on Bobbie's right. They were all sweating, and felt as if they had butterflies flying in their stomachs. Bobbie had to fight a sick feeling to keep from vomiting. They were all dressed in their best suits with white shirts and ties; not at all like disrespectful, juvenile delinquents. The little band of outlaws looked repentant and timid with their long, sad faces. Judge Betts almost felt sorry for them, but restrained the feeling easily and opened the session. "Officers Russo and Slovik, have you anything to add to your reports?"

Officer Russo, sitting on the Judge's right, answered for both, "No, your honor."

The judge turned toward the boys. "The officers charge you boys with breaking and entry and with attempted robbery. I've examined their report fully and accept it as testimony for this hearing." Looking at Miss Kelly, who was seated next to Officer Slovik, Judge Betts continued speaking, "Miss Kelly, your report on the Lee boy was excellent. I'm considering your recommendation."

Martha Kelly loved the official air of a court hearing and couldn't resist voicing a comment. "Your honor, may I make one comment in addition to my report?"

"Yes, you may."

"Your honor, since Bobbie Lee was receiving under the Home Life Assistance Program, and if my recommendation is accepted, he will have to be committed by the court to the state's Guardianship Program or put on the state administered Federal Care Program, which can be done by anyone filing an application in his interest. The result would be the same, placement in a foster home in a rural or suburban area."

"Yes, I'm aware of the prospects from your report," the Judge replied. He looked beyond those seated at the table and addressed the assembled parents. "Where were you parents, when these boys were out at all hours, breaking into gas stations and running the streets late at night?"

This was his usual opening statement to wayward parents of wayward children. Judge Betts believed delinquent parents should be penalized along with their children. He believed children needed strict parental supervision as well as parental love. The judge continued

87

to flay the parents, "If you parents stayed home more . . . supervised your children properly . . . worried less about yourselves and paid more attention to their behavior, you wouldn't be here now!" His complexion was becoming ruddier, his voice growing in volume. "Training children begins in the home; not in the schools! It's your responsibility to raise your children to respect the law and private property! It's not the school's or the police!"

The parents were becoming embarrassed and squirmed nervously in their seats under the vocal blasts from the angry Judge Betts. They were also mad at their children for getting them into this awkward situation. Besides, most of them were losing a day's work.

Judge Betts took a sip of water, paused to let the water wet his parched throat, banged the glass down on the tray, then turned his attention towards the boys. After quickly scanning the reports again, he lifted his head slightly, peering from under his bushy, auburn eyebrows.

"Did you boys think you could go on breaking into gas stations indefinitely?" Not waiting for anyone to answer, he continued, his voice growing in volume, "Did you really think you could get away with breaking the law?" The word, law, echoed off the plaster walls and Judge Betts paused for effect . . . then said, "You boys have shown you can't be trusted to behave yourselves like normal teen-age boys. You need someone watching over you to see that you do what is right!" He stopped. His face was glowing again. He took another sip of water, washed it down slowly, and made another loud return to the tray. Then, he bellowed across the room. "Your parents can't be depended upon to supervise you! They've demonstrated their failure as responsible parents!"

Mr. Higgins winced at the last vocal blast from the seat of justice. A veteran of juvenile hearings, he was

88

aware of the next statement and knew what the decision would be from the tone and trend of the judicial speech.

"I've no alternative, despite Miss Kelly's recommendation for Bobbie Lee, but to commit all five of you to the State Home for Boys at Hainesburg. There, you'll receive the necessary supervision that you aren't getting at home."

The decision made and the sentence past; its impact was felt instantly by everyone in the room, except Mr. Higgins, whose ears were accustomed to such sounds.

The parents were stunned into silence, disbelieving their own hearing. But within a few seconds, there was a stirring of bodies, low-pitched, vocal protests from the men with loud, piercing screams from the women.

Jimmie Heywood's mother leaped to her feet and screamed across the room, "What are ya doin' t' my Jimmie? Please, Judge! Don't take him away from me!" She fell back to her seat and burst into loud sobs. "I'll kill myself!" She sobbed into her hands, covering her face.

This was too much for Judge Betts. He couldn't tolerate this bedlam in his courtroom. He ordered Mr. Higgins and the two staff members standing against the wall; "Remove all parents from the courtroom."

When a respectful decorum was restored to his courtroom, Judge Betts ordered his clerk; "Prepare commitment papers for all five boys." Standing up for the first time, signaling the end of the proceedings, he addressed Mr. Higgins, "You'll wait until the parents have left the building, before you take the boys out of the room. Have them sent to Hainesburg as soon as possible. Tomorrow at the latest. I'll have the court order signed and sent over today."

With that last statement, it was all over. They had been tried and found guilty. The five sullen boys with bent shoulders and moist eyes were led from the room.

Little Jimmie Heywood had tears running down his cheeks, dripping onto the floor. Bobbie felt sick inside. Calvin, Larry and Junior stared at the floor with long-faced pouts. They marched single file down the long corridor, looking like five zombies, wide-eyed and stiff-jointed with shock.

CHAPTER 12

Winter came back in a hurry. The air had suddenly become cold with relentless, gusty winds that penetrated even the heaviest clothing. The temperature was around fifteen above zero and it took over ten minutes to warm the motors of both county cars. Finally, the two-car caravan left the County Youth House parking area, skidding and sliding over icy patches of previously melted snow. The hot exhaust fumes vaporized continuously behind each car in the frigid air, leaving a gray-white trail—a finger-like flag flapping in the wind. Their destination was the State Home for Boys on the outskirts of Hainesburg, New Sussex. A trip calculated to be about twenty miles and some thirty-five minutes of time.

Bobbie and Calvin sat in the rear seat of the first, black, two-door sedan, while Larry, Junior and Jimmie were in the second car. Two county officers sat in the front seat of each car, with the boys' personal gear deposited in the trunks.

Bobbie and Calvin exchanged glances of excitement and fear. They both wore wool suits and heavy wool overcoats, but the car's heater was prematurely broadcasting cool air and it made them shiver. For something to say, Bobbie commented, "Man, it's cold!" His breath vaporized into a gray-white, miniature cloud.

Calvin cupped his hands and blew his warm breath on them. He turned toward Bobbie and asked in a soft, low voice, "Scared?"

Bobbie hesitated, then answered, "No, man, I ain't scared!" He turned away and looked out the window. "Looks like it's gonna snow."

Calvin glanced at Bobbie with a curious expression on his face, but said nothing.

They were on Route One, parallel with Cranston, New Sussex, when the snow started. It added a dreary note to the already foreboding quality of the trip. The boys sensed it. They became silent, almost brooding.

An occasional comment between the officers couldn't subdue the continuous traveling noises: the thump of tires over railroad tracks, the hum of spinning tires on the smooth asphalt and the wind rushing past the windows into the cracks and crevices of the cars.

The scenery was quickly changing from a naked brown bleakness to the snowy bright whiteness of a winter rural scene. Having turned off Route One, they were traveling cautiously on a macadam paved, county road. The snow was swirling and dancing around the spinning wheels. On both sides of the road the fields of winter rye and the earth-brown, barren fields were covered with a coat of clean, fresh, snow. Naked-limbed maples and oaks were made decent again with cottony white garments clinging to their spindly branches.

The rural scene changed to suburban as they approached Hainesburg. The snow was rapidly covering the newly constructed ranchers and cape cods between clumps of empty-limbed trees, promising a return of lush green leaves and refreshing shade from summer's heat. A hillside cemetery on their right was somber and still with its memories and relics buried under the blanketing snow. Its marble and granite monuments were being battered unmercifully. The snowflakes were becoming larger, the snowstorm growing to blizzard force, when they came to the outskirts of Hainesburg.

After the cars thumped over the railroad tracks that dissect the small town of Hainesburg's wide, main street, they made a right turn and climbed a steep incline. At the top of the hill the boys had a good view of the narrow lake below. It looked cold as it lapped at the day's meal; icy flaked crystals of snow. Across the gray-blue lake the sandy beach was empty and uninviting.

The road climbed steadily, passed roadside stores, taverns and houses shut against the storm. Suddenly, before them, a black arrowsign with white letters, pointing down a narrow, hard-surfaced road, announcing the destination—State Home for Boys. A tense feeling collared all five youths. Their steadily mounting fears received a jolt. When they saw the ominous beacon directing them down an unfamiliar road, they suddenly realized how close it was. Jimmie, wide-eyed and almost in tears, kept straining his neck as they drove the final mile. Larry and Junior looked at each other with fear and confusion spreading over their faces. Their mouths were slits of half-smile, half-grin; betraying a self-conscious feeling at their predicament.

Calvin stared at the back of the officer's head in front of him. He thought, "Hope I can take it. Hope I don't bawl like a baby." Embarrassed at his own thoughts, he turned quickly and looked at Bobbie, making sure he hadn't uttered his thoughts. He was relieved, Bobbie was staring at the bleakness and the snowflakes, jetting past the misty, opaque window like tiny racing meteors.

Bobbie was deep in thought; hating the predicament he was in, his mother's death and the fear that was gnawing at him. He hated being afraid. It made him feel uneasy.

The entrance scene was wasted on the five youths. The red brick piers at the entrance, the skeletal trees outlined in white along both sides of the driveway and the beautiful blanket of white snow were given only passing glances by the boys. But they raised their heads and strained their necks to see the windows of the buildings as they circled the campus grounds, heading towards the parking area near the reception cottage.

They were looking for bars on the windows, because they had immature ideas about Hainesburg; thinking it would have barred windows and a high stone fence around it, similar to the somber looking state prison in Mercerton. On numerous occasions they had walked past the high, forbiding, brownstone walls with raised mortar joints and square towers housing alert, armed guards. The relief could be heard from all five boys, when they didn't see any barred windows or stone walls. The open effect of the grounds gave a more favorable, friendly impression, contrasting their preconceived ideas.

Calvin leaned closer to Bobbie and whispered, "Don't look too bad." He paused a second, before asking, "What ya think?"

Bobbie looked relieved. His vision of a rough confinement was eased somewhat, so he quickly changed his opinion of the place. With a relaxed grin on his face, he answered, "Don't look rough. Ain't nothin' like the prison back home."

"That's what I think," Calvin said with his broad, dark brown face breaking into a smile. He added, "Hope we's right."

The county officers delivered the five youths enmasse at the administration building. The snow storm made them hurry, getting all five boys and their gear parked in the waiting room, while their commitment papers were presented for verification of the judge's signature. With the formality accomplished, the officers offered hasty farewells and hurried back to Mercerton, hoping to get there before the main force of the storm struck. Their quick departure left the boys in a void, sitting in the warm, but cheerless reception room with outward patience but inside, they were anxious to become part of the institution. They wanted to be a part of something and the waiting made them feel too transitional to be comfortable or satisfied.

Bobbie and his gang soon became a part of the State Home for Boys, referred to simply as Hainesburg. The routine of the orientation period helped make the first days pass rapidly. At the hospital they were given complete physicals. Each department head gave a lecture about his part in the operation of the institution: the school and work programs, rules, regulations and recreation, down to parole policy. They didn't have time to be homesick, or feel sorry for themselves. The psychological tests, achievement tests, innoculations, a second physical examination and the interviews by the psychologist, educational and counseling staff members were filling the days easily. And the new faces and new personalities in their orientation group were interesting, giving them a chance to exchange experiences.

When the orientation was completed, Bobbie said to himself the night before his assignment to a cottage; "Ain't too bad! I'll make it."

On his day to be reassigned, the reports of the interviews, tests and recommendations were being reviewed by the committee responsible for the placement of each boy to a cottage, school and work assignment. Bobbie Lee's background reports had been read by all five members and they were ready to discuss his situation.

The psychologist summarized his report for the committee:

"It was obvious to me from the interviews, and the

test results corroborated my feelings. This boy was over-compensating against feelings of inferiority and inadequacy. His intelligence is average, his size is below normal for his age group and he exhibits aggressive leadership tendencies. His aggressions are probably of a compensatory nature. He also showed a trait of shrewdness with an acute awareness of his environment. He's capable of assuming a follower role, but given an opportunity, will attempt to assume leadership. His relationship with his mother wasn't satisfactory to him. It appears he was denied a full share of her love and affection. He had to take a secondary position to her lover and other pleasures. This could be a very likely source for his feelings of anxiety, which were evident in the interviews and again corroborated in the personality tests' results. This boy is still malleable, and needs firm supervision combined with affectionate understanding. He needs a good male personality to emulate, and needs to channel his energies toward more beneficial pursuits. The Explorers or Boy Scouts would be good for this boy. An understanding, friendly cottage master would be needed for emulation purposes. That's about it for my summary."

The other four members nodded agreement, then the director of education contributed his recommendations for Bobbie's school placement. "His achievement tests results were below normal for his age group. He would normally be in the ninth grade, but was only in the seventh grade in school. He was weak in most subject areas, and shows a definite need for remedial attention in the verbal area. A placement in grade six in our system would be more in line with his abilities. He isn't ready for a grade seven placement, having had difficulty with the subject matter in the previous school. His caseworker's report obviates my conclusion on that matter. I guess that's about it. Any comments?"

The social worker from the State Commission of Child Welfare had one question. "Was his mathematics score also deficient?"

"Yes, but not as poor as the verbal area."

The classification officer gave his recommendation; "Since he's small, a work assignment on the farm would possibly be too strenuous." After surveying the group, he continued, "An assignment to the cleaning detail wouldn't be too hard for him. I suggest we place him there."

"It sounds all right during winter. But, an outside position would help him develop, physically. I suggest a change to a farm position in the spring. One that wouldn't be too strenuous," the social worker stated.

The classification officer conceded the possible benefits from the change. And the group came to a final decision for a tentative work assignment with the cleaning detail, a sixth grade school assignment and placement in cottage seven, supervised by Mr. Lone Bostick, a firm but fair man with an ability to handle young boys.

Lone Bostick was a former social worker from a northern New Sussex city that had a large Negro population. He had a natural friendly way of handling boys. But after six years of city social work, he decided to try Hainesburg, where he could concentrate his abilities to better advantage. Lone Bostick wanted to help boys from his own race. He felt stifled as a regular caseworker with the usual heavy caseload that all but smothered his efforts. So, he accepted the position of cottage master at Hainesburg and was in his second year, when Bobbie Lee arrived.

Lone Bostick was an average size man, without a lot

of muscle. He had regular Negroid features; dark kinky hair, dark brown skin, a wide nose and a heavy lower lip. He wore black horn-rimmed eyeglasses, and would rather read good fiction and listen to classical music, then play at the more strenuous, outdoor activities; such as golf or tennis.

It was his ability to get young boys to feel at ease in his company that enabled Lone Bostick to accomplish wonders with the difficult, problem youths. They sensed his readiness to listen and understand their feelings. It made them feel important.

CHAPTER 13

Lone Bostick had just finished giving his assistant instructions for the afternoon when Bobbie walked in the front door. Lone let the assistant leave, then walked out of the recreation room to greet Bobbie. "Hi, Bobbie!" Lone smiled and offered his right hand.

Bobbie shook Lone's hand and looked up at the medium-size man with the medium-size build. He said to himself, "He's colored!" Then he returned the greeting, "'lo, Mr. Bostick."

"Just leave your bags, Bobbie. We'll take care of them." Lone leaned toward the recreation room's door and said, "Jack, come out here, please." Jack turned out to be a thin, bony, white boy with mousy brown hair and a pale, sad face. "Jack, this is Bobbie." Jack nodded at Bobbie, who nodded back at Jack. "Take Bobbie's bags, please, while I show him around." Jack responded silently, while Lone said, "Thank you, Jack," as the youth walked down the long, wide hall.

Lone put a friendly arm around Bobbie's narrow shoulders. "Let's take a look at the place, okay?"

Bobbie nodded, but kept silent. With Lone Bostick's arm around Bobbie's shoulders they walked into the recreation room, through the two long sleeping rooms and both lavatories on the first floor; the shower and dressing rooms in the basement and even inspected Lone's private quarters upstairs..

Bobbie's nervous stomach calmed down, after the

friendly reception from Mr. Bostick. When he learned about the separation of the gang that morning and his placement in Mr. Bostick's cottage, he became upset. Bobbie had a difficult time digesting his food and the anxious chatter during breakfast added to his stomach troubles. He was glad when it was over, and they had finally gone back to the reception cottage. Packing his clothes for the short trip across the campus grounds, kept him busy and reduced conversation to a minimum; the comments and endless questions by Jimmie and the others. Bobbie didn't have the answers, and he wasn't in the mood to invent them. He just wanted to pack, separate and get the change of quarters over with. New situations always made him feel queasy inside. But once he made the first step of adjustment, he would begin to relax and gradually get used to it. Then he would change things to suit him, if possible.

Of all the boys that he met that first day, Bobbie was impressed with only one. An older, Negro youth of sixteen, whose name was Rayford Elston. Rayford played the role of the "cool one." He was considered a sharp talker and the most worldly. He had done just about everything, so he said, and his slow, confident way of talking made you believe him. Being the natural leader of the boys, everyone paid homage to his commands. Rayford was the strongest and toughest boy in the cottage. No one challenged his unwritten title.

Bobbie and Rayford became friends from their first meeting. It was a mutual attraction. Bobbie was delighted, when his bunk was placed next to Rayford's. He was already forgetting about his old gang and looking forward to the new friendship, even if he had to play a disciple role. Rayford, the "cool one," made it easy for him to give up the leadership role. Bobbie had at last found someone he could admire and copy from his "world."

The first night, after lights were out, Bobbie and Rayford lay awake and compared notes. "Where ya from, Bobbie?" Rayford asked with his calm, melodious voice.

"From Mercerton."

"No kiddin', man, Mercerton?"

"Yeah, South Mercerton. Alliance Street."

"Ain't that somethin'. Me, too," Rayford declared, the words sliding slowly off his tongue.

Bobbie rolled on his side and faced Rayford in the dark. He said with an excited shrill in his voice, "What part, Rayford?"

"East Mercerton, man—Pierson Street."

"Where's Pierson Street?"

"Off No'th Fenton," Rayford replied. "Know where No'th Fenton is don't ya?"

"Yeah, but ain't never heard of Pierson Street."

"Come around Joe's Luncheonette on No'th Fenton, man. Show ya around. Let ya meet some tough studs."

"I'll be 'round," Bobbie said, a determined tone in his voice. After a short pause, he asked, "How long ya been here, Rayford?"

"Man, been here five months. Gettin' tired, too. Can't wait t' get back on the block."

"What's the block?"

"Man, ya know, back on the co'ner . . . back home . . . where I can get me some wine an' reefers. . . . Get me some nice broads," Rayford said; unseen in the dark a smile parted his thick lips.

Bobbie kept silent. He only had a vague idea of these pleasures with an occasional cigarette and childish sex play to his credit. The big things in life had yet to be experienced. He just lay there, quietly admiring Rayford and his experiences. That first night set the pattern for Bobbie's relationship with Rayford. They became not only close friends but teacher and student; Bobbie, the eager student, Rayford, the willing teacher.

The weeks passed rapidly into early spring. Bobbie was by now an accepted member of the cottage and Rayford's official protege. This entitled him to respect and a "hands-off" policy; no rough stuff from the older, bigger boys in the cottage. Bobbie enjoyed his position, taking advantage of it on work details by letting his partner of the day do the more difficult part and most of the assigned cleaning jobs.

"Tommy, do them windas on that side. I'll get 'em at this end."

"Only two windles on your end. I'll be doin' five," Tommy Byrnes protested in a high-pitched voice. His face wrinkled into a pained expression. Tommy's cheeks became pink and his small ears reddened, also. He left his mouth open with yellow-white buckteeth sticking out.

"Want me t' tell Rayford?"

After Tommy thought over Bobbie's last statement, he replied, "All right, don't say nothin' to Rayford." Tommy stared with sad blue eyes at his dull brown shoes. His buckteeth hung over his lower lip like a beaver ready to chew on a tree.

Bobbie smiled, then walked to his two windows, laughing to himself.

When Bobbie would meet one of the "old" gang in the mess hall or on work details, it would be a friendly meeting. They would talk as long as possible, but he knew that when he was released, it wouldn't be the same with the others. He was already looking forward to being back on the "block" with Rayford, enjoying the big pleasures Rayford promised; and one of these was smoking.

Though Bobbie had tried smoking before, he never formed the habit. With Rayford's help he became a steady smoker. He could inhale without becoming sick or dizzy.

At first Bobbie wondered where they got the cigarettes, since they weren't sold at the campus store. He soon found out. They got them on their visits into town; an incentive offered for good behavior by the institution. There was a regular and active trading market in cigarettes and by the end of March, Bobbie was active in it, also.

When the first day of April arrived, it was cool, but had a promise of warmth. The sky was lake blue with fair-weather puffs of white floating overhead. The wind was gentle. Long thin branches with tiny young buds swayed gently in the cool, steady breeze. For recreation period, the entire cottage group was outside on the playground area enjoying the day. Mr. Bostick and his assistant were umpiring the softball game. Bobbie, Rayford and two other boys were playing quoits, nearby. It was a relaxing, calming day. The kind that made you glad to be alive, able to see, smell, and feel the newness of spring. You could taste the freshness of spring in the wind, everytime you opened your mouth to speak.

Bobbie and Rayford won the game and they were giving their two losers some friendly harassment. Taking a rest, they sat down on the cottage porch and began discussing one of the favorite topics of the older boys—girls. "Had me a nice broad, night befo' we got caught." Rayford's mouth opened wide and his eyes bulged, thinking about it. Sex was the one thing that made Rayford get excited. He would lose his usual calmness and slow speech, getting excited in voice and gestures.

William Lance, one of the older youths, who was in for attempted rape, asked Rayford, "Give ya a lotta action?"

"Man, rode on her fo' twen'y minutes, befo' I popped my cookies." He laughed, injecting his entire body into the scene.

"Where'd ya lay her?" asked Joseph Cunningham, who was sitting next to Bobbie. His acne-covered face wrinkled with the question, making his puffy nose look more swollen. Cunningham's straight flaxen hair lay across his pimply forehead, and slits of gray peeped out between heavy eyelids.

"Man, had her in a car—on the back seat. One of my buddy's had her girl friend on the front seat. Both goin' like two jack-hammers. Man, did that car shake! Almost got seasick!" It broke them up. They became four falling bodies, bumping into each other and laughing out loud.

After they had calmed down and sat down again on the wooden steps, Rayford asked Bobbie, "Ever been laid, Bobbie?"

Bobbie was embarrassed, but he wouldn't lie to Rayford, . . . "No, man, ain't never been laid!"

"That's all right, Bobbie. When we get out, I'll fix ya up. Get ya a lotta pussy!" Rayford put his arm around Bobbie and gave him a light, affectionate punch on his chest.

Bobbie kept quiet. He just sat there and grinned at Rayford. Bobbie knew he could depend on Rayford.

Besides enjoying himself with Rayford, Bobbie was also doing well in school. He was in the slow reading group in his class, but didn't mind. He liked the attention he got in this group. Their teacher, Mr. Mark Thompson, wasn't a stern man and he never ridiculed anyone for their mistakes. He was one of the few teachers in the school that could maintain discipline through personal respect. He seldom used force or threats, but the boys in the class knew that he couldn't be pushed around.

In contrast to a usual serious expression, Mark Thompson had a friendly smile and a pleasant way of laughing. When a situation became humorous, and the class had a good laugh, he would join in with a baritone chuckle or two. But always demanded good, middle-class manners and if anyone broke a rule, they were corrected on the spot.

"What was our rule about speaking in class?" Mr. Thompson asked the boy sitting behind Bobbie. Mark Thompson's face became a study in line and shape; straight nose and even jaw lines meeting at an even point below straight, even, thin lips.

"Not to interrupt, Wait 'til the speaker is finished."

"What do you do, when you want to contribute?" Mark Thompson stared at the boy, his dark brown pupils, contrasting with their clear white backgrounds.

"Excuse yourself first."

"Are you going to interrupt anymore?"

"No, sir!"

"I'm glad to hear that, Ronald, I know you have better manners. I'm glad you're going to cooperate." Mark Thompson's face relaxed into a friendly expression.

Bobbie was in Mr. Thompson's class in the morning and he liked the idea of half-day sessions. School didn't bore him, now. He had made more progress in the three months at Hainesburg, than the previous three years in school.

"That was very good, Bobbie. You didn't mispronounce any words. You read all the punctuation signs correctly. You'll soon be ready for group B."

105

Bobbie smiled down at his book, feeling satisfied at his progress. This was the first time that he ever enjoyed reading. It didn't seem like drudgery or a nuisance to be endured. He liked being told about his progress and felt confident in Mr. Thompson's class.

It was unfortunate that Mr. Thompson, who made a favorable impression with Bobbie, only had him for a few hours a day; Monday through Friday. Mr. Bostick was another favorable influence, but having only one assistant on duty at a time, he wasn't able to give enough of himself to each boy. His cottage was overcrowded and his time was limited for individual contacts. He had to do most of his work through group situations.

But Rayford and the two older youths, William Lance and Joe Cunningham, had all the time necessary for molding and shaping a youth like Bobbie Lee, who wasn't quite fifteen years old.

"Ever steal a car, Bobbie?" asked William Lance, while they were sitting at supper together. Lance was a heavy-set Negro adolescent with an extremely fat face that was almost featureless, except for a pair of circular nostrils and thick, extended lips. His black eyes could hardly be seen behind his fat eyelids.

"No, man, not me!"

"It's easy, Bobbie, All ya gotta do is jump the ignition wires under the dashboard," William Lance replied, his mouth opened into a wide wet smile, revealing two empty spaces in his front teeth.

"That's how come I'm here," Rayford said, chewing his words with a mouthful of food. "Jumped one too many ignition wires."

They all had a good laugh on Rayford, who laughed the hardest.

"I'd like t' drive," Bobbie replied. He put his fork

down, picked up his cloth napkin and wiped his mouth. "How ol' ya gotta be?"

Rayford answered, "Seventeen." He laughed to himself, then said to the others, while gazing at his piece of apple pie, "If ya got nerve like me, don't wait 'til then. Was drivin' when I was fo'teen." Rayford tilted his head to the right and looked at the others with half-closed black eyes. His thick lips parted in a sly grin.

Bobbie looked at Rayford and the smug expression on his face. He asked, "Gonna teach me, when we gets out?"

"Sure, man, we'll have a ball!" Rayford reached across the table, and stole a forkful of ice cream from Joe Cunningham's plate with a sudden, deft thrust. Joe looked surprised. His stuttering, vocal complaint added to the scene. Everyone laughed. Even Joe Cunningham laughed, to show Rayford he wasn't mad at him.

Rayford's friendship helped the days mesh into an even flow of time, but even his constant influence didn't make up for the loss of Bobbie's mother. Bobbie missed her most on visiting days, when the other boys were seeing their relatives. This was maturing one aspect of his personality. He would have been content to see her, even if she came with Joe Wilson. Bobbie was glad when visiting days were over. They always made him feel funny inside; an empty, lonely feeling.

CHAPTER 14

The basement shower room provided a study in contrasts: Bobbie's small, thin, wiry torso against his shower mate's tall, thick, well-proportioned body; Bobbie's brown skin against Rayford's dark brown hue; Rayford's jovial mood contrasting Bobbie's quiet, thoughtful mood. The sharp sting of the cold shower had felt good to Rayford, and he dried himself with brisk arm motions. Bobbie dabbed himself dry with a listless effort.

"Can't believe it, Bobbie!" Rayford shouted, throwing the wet towel on the concrete floor. "Got me my walkin' papers!"

The institution's policy and decision making Board of Managers had notified the cottage which boys were being paroled that month, subject to supervision by the State's Central Parole Bureau. Rayford Elston was included in the group from their cottage.

Rayford still hadn't recovered his usual "cool" exterior. He was jubilant, and the more he laughed and joked, the more it depressed Bobbie. Rayford was too happy to notice Bobby's silence.

"When we get upstairs, give ya my address. Write me, when ya get out," Rayford said, while slipping into a pair of tan, summer-weight trousers.

"Not gonna fo'get me, are ya Rayford?"

"No, man, ya know I ain't!"

"I'll write ya befo' I gets out. Okay?" Bobbie continued buttoning his shirt, and stared intently at his progress.

"Write ya soon's I can. Keep ya posted on what's happenin'." Rayford's face beamed his thoughts. He allowed himself to smile.

They finished dressing and walked upstairs. Rayford had his right arm around Bobbie's shoulder. Bobbie asked, as they climbed the last few steps, "Gonna let me help pack?"

"I'm no good at packin'." Laughing and giving Bobbie a tug at the shoulder, Rayford confided, "Need ya t'keep me from goofin'."

While Bobbie was helping Rayford pack, he was counting the months he'd been in Hainesburg. "Over six months, already!" he said to himself. Bobbie thought about the first days in the reception cottage, and could only remember them vaguely. They seemed like an eternity ago. He wondered about the time that he still had to do, recalling his tentative release date was supposed to have been one day last month—in July. Rayford's release made Bobby want to get out now—not two months later. He could actually feel the yearning, deep inside his stomach. The thought of spending more unending months, made his stomach feel like it was twisting into a knot. Bobbie felt a sharp pain everytime he bent over, and knew it was going to be a rough night getting to sleep. He wasn't looking forward to it or towards tomorrow morning either.

Rayford stood next to his luggage on the porch steps, while he shook hands with the boys as they left the cottage for school or work details that morning.

When Bobbie's turn came, he offered Rayford his small, delicate hand. It was dwarfed in Rayford's extremely wide mitt. They smiled at each other, and Bobbie spoke first. "Be seein' ya."

"You bet. Keep cool." Rayford looked at Bobbie from

underneath heavy eyelids. After a second handshake, he said, "Be waitin' for ya."

They looked at each other for a few seconds, without speaking, then Rayford picked up his bags and left.

Bobbie stood on the top step, watching Rayford amble towards the administration building to wait for his brother, who was taking him back to Mercerton. "Back home," Bobbie sighed.

Silently, Bobbie appreciated Rayford's last, over-the-shoulder glance and arm wave. He waved back. But it couldn't relieve the tight feeling in his throat. The sudden thought that Rayford had a home, made him wonder about his own situation. Where could he go, when he was paroled? Who was going to take care of him? Bobbie tried to remember what his mother looked like. Her memory was already becoming vague, along with the memories of the apartment. Tears began sliding down his face, before he became conscious of them. He wiped the tears away, relieved that no one had seen him cry.

Bobbie's tight, pinchy throat made him feel uncomfortable during the oral reading session in school that morning, but he survived, without permanent injury. After the noon meal, it became apparent to Bobbie he was on his own; no Rayford to support him. He began maneuvering for the cottage power position. His methods were different, but the goal was the same—leadership. Bobbie was gradually replacing his brassy, loud, bluffing methods for a more indirect, subtle and outwardly friendly approach. He was developing his own brand of successful charm.

The official head of the cottage was Lone Bostick with the assistant on duty, next in command. But the unofficial leaders of the cottage were in control as a three-man ruling body: Joseph Cunningham, William Lance and

Bobbie Lee. Bobbie, as Rayford's protege, inherited his vacated leadership position but didn't complain about sharing it with Cunningham and Lance, who were tough and had seniority. Cunningham and Lance didn't protest Bobbie's taking Rayford's place. They expected it.

Bobbie's new leadership position was useful. It made life as easy as possible in the cottage but it was a poor substitute for his real desire; a big slice of freedom back on the block with Rayford. So, he marked time, counted the days and held on miserably until parole day. It was slow in coming.

Before he left Hainesburg, two interesting events happened to his partners-in-leadership, leaving him in position to take over as leader in the cottage.

Joe Cunningham got involved in two scrapes; one with another boy in the cottage and another with one of the assistants. This was enough to get him into the segregation shack, known officially as the guidance unit. He had to leave the cottage completely to live in the segregation shack under the supervision of the instructor counselors, whose job was to help boys learn how to get along with others at Hainesburg.

William Lance was paroled in September, after Joe Cunningham's departure, leaving the entire command to Bobbie. Quick to take advantage, Bobbie immediately looked over the cottage for prospects. He needed a strong cohort. So, he picked the most reserved, but strongest boy in the cottage as his second-in-command, but actually more of a strong-arm assistant. This solved the power problem in case anyone tried to argue the point. Control of the cottage would remain with him until he gladly gave it up on parole day. It couldn't come too soon for him.

Bobbie received the coveted news early in October. He was being paroled to the community, under the dual supervision of the Central Parole Bureau and the State Commission of Child Welfare. Miss Kelly's recommendation for placement under the state's guardianship, because of his mother's death and the lack of interested relatives, had been accepted by the Juvenile Court Judge. His commitment to the state's guardianship had been ordered by the court. He was to be placed in a foster home.

Bobbie didn't realize what it would mean to be under the state and live in a foster home. He was too happy to worry about it. His terse comment, "Feel real good!" expressed his feelings on the matter.

CHAPTER 15

With his bags stored in the trunk, the fairwells over with, Bobbie was eager for travel. Impatient, he kept looking towards the office door, while he sat waiting in the black sedan with the state's gold seal on each door. Finally, the state social worker, a Mr. Norman Messner, came out of the office. He entered the car, started the motor and drove it around the main administrative building, deftly and without comment.

Bobbie was surprised to see a male social worker. His idea of a social worker was strictly female. A man in an unusual position piqued his curiosity. Bobbie studied him closely, trying to remember his name at the same time. His brown wavy hair was combed straight back. He had a firm chin, a long, prominent nose that came downward out of a strong, prominent forehead and had a dark, white man's tan, that intrigued Bobbie, who wanted to talk to this well-dressed, intent young man.

They navigated the tree-lined, macadam roadway, paused between the red brick entrance piers and waited for a car on the right to drive pass. Bobbie turned around and glanced back for his last look. The scene was a lot different from nine months ago.

Early autumn in New Sussex is still warm with green-leafed trees and bushes shading to tints of red, yellow and orange. A languid haziness hangs in the air, during this brief, pleasant time known as Indian Summer.

Bobbie's last look was behind him now, with the nine-month block of time locked in his memory. He was matured in many ways and he knew it. He gazed out the car's window at the rural harvest scene: endless rows of stacked cornstalks; pickers bent over in potato fields searching for the last of the dusty tubers; next to fields with fat, orange pumpkins waiting patiently for Halloween.

Bobbie decided to start the conversation. He wanted to know more about his new foster home. "Where's Lawnside Avenue, sir?" he asked, avoiding the forgotten name with sir.

"In Laurelton Township, Bobbie." Norman Messner's voice was baritone, his speech clipped and neat.

"Near Mercerton?"

"Right next to it."

Not satisfied with the answer, Bobbie pressed for a more exact location. "How far from Mercerton?"

"Not too far—just off Laurelton Road. Ever been on the Laurelton Road?" Mr. Messner asked, looking at Bobbie for the first time.

"No," Bobbie answered and looked into Norman Messner's large brown eyes.

"It's only a few miles from downtown Mercerton."

This was the answer Bobbie was hoping for. It told him East Mercerton wasn't too far away. He could still get to see Rayford.

"Colored folks?"

"Yes. And they're interested in helping boys get a new start. They're very nice people."

Bobbie looked directly at him and asked, "Other boys in the home?"

"Two."

"Colored?"

"Yes. Around your age," Mr. Messner answered, then checked both directions, before turning left into the main highway, heading towards Mercerton.

The change in direction stopped the conversation temporarily, allowing Bobbie enough time to assemble a new set of questions. He opened the second round of conversation. "Gonna be my case worker?"

"Yes, but don't forget you're going to have a parole officer, too."

"Where's his office, Mercerton?"

"Yes. You'll report to him every month.. He'll also visit at the foster home. He'll want to know how you're doing." He paused and looked at Bobbie with a lined brow, unconsciously arching his thick brown eyebrows. "If you get in trouble, he'll send you back to Hainesburg. Better behave yourself in school. Don't hang around with the wrong kind of boys!"

Bobbie thought about Mr. Messner's advice, and wondered if he could take going back to Hainesburg. He decided that he would have to be extra careful, now that he was going to be watched. Bobbie had confidence in Rayford. He knew Rayford was also on parole, and would be watched like him. He said to himself, "I can depend on Rayford. He's smart. Won't let us get hung-up again." Bobbie returned to the conversation and he opened part three by asking, "Gonna be checkin' on me, too?"

"Yes, I'll be visiting the home."

"What's their names? Fo'got them."

"Younger—Mr. and Mrs. Elias Younger."

"What do I call them?"

"You'll have to work that out with them, Bobbie."

"What school do I go to?"

"Junior high.".

115

"In Mercerton?"

"No, Laurelton Township. It's a new school. You'll like it better than the one in Mercerton."

"Hope so."

Norman Messner looked at the passing scenery and announced, "Don't have far to go. Should be there in about five minutes."

Lawnside Avenue was a tree-shaded, narrow, one-way suburban street with the houses set close to the sidewalks. The Younger home was at the extreme end of the street on the westerly side. It stood alone with vacant ground on both sides. Its clapboard was covered with faded green paint. The front porch had wood paneled sides, three feet high, supporting four, round, wood pillars which in turn supported a slanting roof.

When they drove into the Younger's dirt driveway, the tires skidded, before stopping completely. Bobbie and Mr. Messner lurched forward then backward to a normal sitting position. When they got out of the car, Bobbie joined Mr. Messner at the rear trunk to help unload the baggage. Before the last suitcase was taken out of the trunk, they heard a friendly, "Hello, didn't expect you this soon!" coming from the nearby sidewalk. Surprised, they looked up to see a graying, middle-aged, neatly dressed, Negro matron.

She walked over to them and introduced herself to Bobbie. "How do you do young man, I'm Mrs. Younger." Sara Younger extended her thin, long-fingered, right hand towards Bobbie, who shook it lightly.

"Mrs. Younger, this is Bobbie Lee," Mr. Messner said, assuming the introduction duties. "May we carry his bags in now?" he asked, anxious to get the placement completed.

"Oh, yes! Just take them in through the front," Sara Younger replied with her soprano voice.

Mr. Messner handed a suitcase to Bobbie and grabbed the other three, hoping to hurry the baggage transfer. He almost tripped on the last step, but managed to deposit everything in good condition on the brown and white, oval-shaped, braided rug.

They faced each other across the small pile of traveling gear, an awkward moment passed before Mr. Messner said, "Shall we carry the bags upstairs?"

"The bags can wait. Bobbie and I can get acquainted over lunch, first." Sara Younger put her thin, delicate fingers on Bobbie's arm. "Would you like to see your room?" Mrs. Younger smiled, her bow-shaped lips parted, revealing two rows of white, even teeth. She had sparkling brown eyes set far apart, that seemed to flutter and dance when she smiled. Sara Younger was still an attractive woman.

Bobbie was slightly embarrassed. He wasn't use to strange adults giving him their complete attention and answered, "Yes!" The physical action would be a refreshing pause. It would give him time to get use to this new world.

The stairs creaked slightly like tired crickets as they walked up them and entered a neat, completely furnished bedroom. The two adults stood quietly aside, while Bobbie stared silently around the room.

"Mrs. Younger looked down at Bobbie and asked, "Like your bedroom?"

"It's nice." After a slight pause, Bobbie decided he better add to his short statement. "Gonna like it fine!" Remembering the other boys, Bobbie asked, "Where the other boys sleep?"

"They have their own rooms, Bobbie. This old house has lots of room!" Sara Younger smiled, as she made a sweeping arm movement to emphasize her last statement. Her narrow, small nose widened at the nostrils, when she smiled and her small, round face conveyed a friendly offer to see the other rooms.

Mrs. Younger led them out of the bedroom to see the rest of the second floor. They went downstairs and toured the first floor. Bobbie and Mrs. Younger said good-bye to Mr. Messner, then went into the kitchen for lunch.

After the friendly, get-acquainted conversation with Mrs. Younger, Bobbie was relieved to be alone. He unpacked his clothes and put them away, while looking over the redecorated bedroom: the pastel-blue walls, white wood trim, the white furniture with gold decals and the blue bedspread with white decorative fringe. The room had a clean smell, blending with the present, faint odor of paint. To Bobbie, this room was a sanctuary. He was pleased. His face relaxed into a smile when he looked at himself in the mirror that was hanging on the wall above the dresser. He had enough of dormatory-style living at Hainesburg.

Bobbie's privacy was shattered when Mrs. Younger announced, "Bobbie, supper is ready." Bobbie had been staring blankly at the ceiling, while lying on the bed in his shorts and tee shirt but sat up and answered, "Be right down." He slipped on tan pants and a brown sleeveless summer shirt, then walked down the stairs slowly, his progress marked by each creaking step.

Bobbie stood in the archway between the living room and the dining room, and looked at the three male strangers; two adolescents and one adult. Mrs. Younger sprang out of her chair, and hurried around the rectangular-shaped kitchen table. She placed her arm around

Bobbie's shoulder, escorting him to his seat and didn't introduce him to her husband or the two boys, Donald Jacks and Milton Green, until he was seated.

"I'll prepare your platter for you, Bobbie," Mrs. Younger volunteered. "Do you like gravy on your meat?"

"Yes."

"Peas and mashed potatoes?"

"Yes."

"Salad?"

"Yes."

What would you like to drink?"

"Soda."

"We've only got root beer. Will that be alright?"

"I like root beer."

Silence again, except for chewing sounds.

Trying to be friendly and natural, Mr. Younger attempted conversation. "Bobbie, do you like football?"

"Like basketball better." Bobbie studied the meat on his plate.

Mr. Younger rubbed his graying, curly hair with his free right hand, looked at the fork in his left hand, then said, "While you're waiting for basketball season, you could come with me and the boys and see some good football games. Think you'd like that?" His dark brown eyes searched Bobbie in detail.

"Guess so. . . don't know much 'bout football."

"Oh, we'll teach you all the rules, Bobbie. Don't worry about that!" Mr. Younger glanced at the two boys to his left. "Won't we boys?" They answered, "Yes," without looking up from their plates. Mr. Younger was satisfied, so he relaxed and returned to his food. He lifted a large piece ofbeef to his mouth and chewed noisily. Elias Younger's features were more Negroid than his wife's. He had a wider nose, brown complexion and thicker lips, and his long chin and wide jaw moved rapidly as he chewed the beef.

Bobbie was famished. He asked for seconds on everything and Mrs. Younger was glad for the activity. Bobbie's request for seconds caused another awkward, silent period, while he attended hungrily to his food, without paying any attention to the others.

They sat quietly for a long time, listening to the sounds and looking at the small figure devour his food, obviously enjoying every mouthful.

Mrs. Younger was unable to endure another second of silence. With a hint of embarrassment in her voice, her light tan skin revealing a slight flush, beginning in her cheeks and runing down her neck, she said, "You boys clear the table, I'll set the dessert dishes?" Looking at Bobbie, she said, "You keep on eating Bobbie. By the time dessert's served, I'm sure you'll be finished." Sara Younger switched her attention to her husband, and said with an air of command as he tried to rise and offer a helping hand; "Keep Bobbie company, while we take the dishes to the kitchen."

Bobbie continued eating through the noisy transfer of dishes and silverware, never lifting his head to acknowledge Mr. Younger's company-keeping presence.

After flag-like slices of chocolate, vanilla and strawberry ice cream were served, consumed and the dining room table cleared, Mrs. Younger steered everyone into the living room for a family-get-acquainted-chat, since supper's conversation was meager. Bobbie sat on the brown single chair. It was comfortably stuffed, even if slightly worn in the arms. Milton and Donald sat on the long beige sofa, while Mr. and Mrs. Younger sat together in the new, pastel-green love seat in the opposite corner facing Bobbie's chair. The battle lines drawn, the "friendly

chat" began with the light artillery. Mrs. Younger tried
one for effect: "Did you have a nice ride down, Bobbie?"
She smiled and waited for a reply.

Bobbie hesitated but finally answered, "Wasn't hot . . .
Jes right fo' ridin'."

"That's good." Then she dropped the bracket round:
"You surprised me, coming before noon. Hadn't expected
you until around two." She continued smiling. "It was
a pleasant surprise that turned out just fine, didn't it,
Bobbie?"

"Yes, mam." Bobbie studied the worn arms of the
chair.

"Did Mr. Messner say you'll be goin' to the junior
high school, Bobbie?" Mr. Younger asked. He rubbed the
arm of the love seat with long, full fingers. Elias Younger
was beginning to put on weight.

"Yes, sir, gonna start Monday," Bobbie replied looking
at the circular designs in the brown and white rug in the
center of the floor.

"That's good. You can go with Donald." Seeking
Donald's agreement, Mr. Younger turned his attention
towards him and asked, "You'll show Bobbie around the
new school, won't you, Donald?" He straightened the
arm cover and waited for a reply.

"Yes, sir." Donald Jacks answered. Never quite getting
used to calling Mr. Younger, dad, he used, sir, whenever
possible.

"What grade Bobbie?" Mr. Younger continued rubbing
the arm of the love seat.

"Gonna try me out in seventh," Bobbie replied.

The "friendly chat" continued between awkward, silent periods. Mrs. Younger glared at Donald and Milton.
"Aren't helping at all. Seems like they don't want another
boy in the house," she said to herself.

121

Deciding to get down to business, Mrs. Younger moved the heavy artillery into position and commenced firing. Without smiling, she said, "Now, Bobbie, you're welcome to stay as long as you like. But we do have to understand each other." She paused to check for effect, studying Bobbie's face but couldn't detect any reaction on his blank expression. She continued; "Everybody has to live by some rules. A few necessary ones can make life a lot nicer. First of all, we won't tolerate any sassy back talk or bad manners. There's no excuse for it." She paused again and studied Bobbie's blank face. "Our bodies need rest so everyone should be in bed by nine during school days and ten on weekends and holidays."

Bobbie looked as though he was paying attention during the rules and regulations barrage, but was actually thinking out ways to evade these necessary observances. He had to stop thinking, and give a confirming reply to a question by Mrs. Younger.

"No, Mrs. Younger, don't think yo' bein' too stric'. Gonna get 'long jes fine. Won't have no trouble." Completely "conned" by the answer, she continued her lecture about his future life in the Younger household. Bobbie even agreed to regular Sunday church attendance; something he never did with his mother. He knew when to give the right answers.

CHAPTER 16

Bobbie had decided to look things over, before attempting to contact Rayford. He knew his caseworker and parole officer would be visiting soon, checking on his adjustment in the Younger home. And Bobbie wasn't looking forward to those dreary, monthly reporting sessions at the parole office, either. He knew Mrs. Younger would report everything to anybody in authority, and he needed time to watch his two foster brothers to see if they could be trusted.

This was to be the pattern of the rapidly maturing Bobbie Lee. He didn't know the meaning of the word impulsive, but he did know that action without planning could be disastrous—disaster in his case, being an immediate return trip to Hainesburg or some other reformatory. So, he decided to give them a favorable image.

Bobbie did all his assigned chores without complaint. He was friendly with Donald, but developed a cool feeling towards Milton. His indifference to the dominated Mr. Younger was almost obvious. Bobbie had difficulty being tolerant towards him.

A week after Bobbie was in the Younger home, Mr. Messner made a surprise visit. It was almost 4:00 p.m. and Bobbie had just arrived from school. After polite inquiries about Bobbie's welfare, Mr. Messner offered his services.

Bobbie was quick to take advantage, asking in a quiet, sincere voice; "Like t' see my mother's grave. Would ya take me?" He stared at Mr. Messner, waiting for his reaction.

The request almost startled Norman Messner but he recovered his composure and answered, "I guess it can be arranged."

"Like t' see it soon, Mr. Messner!"

"Well, since you're anxious, tomorrow would be all right with me." After a quick mental check of his weekly schedule, he confirmed the date. "I'll visit at school. We'll go from there. All right with you, Bobbie?"

"Be fine."

"Good, see you tomorrow at school."

Mr. Messner kept his promise; taking Bobbie to the cemetery, which was about two miles from the Younger home in LaureltonTownship. It had a well manicured lawn, a deep lush-green from the recent rain. There were only seven headstones in the section the attendant located for them. They found the small, rectangular slab of dull-gray granite with the familiar name: Lottie Mae Lee, born, May 7, 1924 died, December 13, 1958.

Bobbie was quiet and still, while he gazed steadily at the headstone, and the blanket of dark green grass. He tried to remember in detail what his mother looked like; closed his eyes to blot out the sun, hoping for a clear image. Mr. Messner stood a respectful distance behind Bobbie, professionally aloof.

He gave up. He could only conjure a vague, mental picture of his mother. She was now a shadow from his past life. "Ain't no use," he thought. "Can't go back. She's dead."

Bobbie stepped away from the grass covered grave that was bare of flowers. He turned to his right and walked past Mr. Messner, heading towards the car.

Bobbie made a vow as he opened the door, "Gonna get Joe Wilson."

During the return trip to the Younger's home, Bobbie sat quietly. It was a content sort of quiet. He now had a goal—the destruction of Joe Wilson.

Bobbie soon discovered who was the favorite in the Younger household. He and Milton were in front of the bathroom, arguing about bathing privileges. "Got here first! Takin' my bath first!" Bobbie shouted, feeling the flush rising upwards from his neck to his face.

"Think so, sonny!" Milton said with a sarcastic stare down his long, broad nose. His cheeks lifted and his wide mouth opened into a defiant sneer. Milton was tall and muscular and towered over Bobbie. The bar of soap was dwarfed in his large right hand, and he tugged at the bright yellow towel around his neck with his equally large left hand.

The conversation became loud, building toward a physical climax. Donald ran downstairs to warn Mrs. Younger, who hurried upstairs immediately. She reached the top of the stairs out of breath, and had to stop, breathing heavily to get her breath back. Her composure regained, she stepped between the two angry boys to prevent a fight.

Sara Younger's final decision was, from Bobbie's standpoint, a personal affront. After she had listened to both versions, she concluded the argument with a final decision; it was apparent from her voice and manner. "Now, Bobbie, Milton's got a very important engagement tonight. Besides, he's the oldest. He's been here the longest. I should think that gives him privileges!" She turned away from Bobbie, addressing Milton with obvious affection, "Milton, take your bath, you haven't time to waste." She returned to Bobbie and ordered, "Bobbie, wait in your room until Milton's done, then you can take your bath."

Bobbie refused to acknowledge her decision. He pivoted on his heels in disgust and walked towards his room, his old strut noticeable. He was growing to dislike that woman.

Mrs. Younger watched Bobbie walk away from her with that arrogant air. She thought to herself, "That boy needs to be taught respect, and I'm the one to do it, too!" She went downstairs, leaving Donald standing alone at the closed bathroom door listening to the noisy, splashing sounds vibrating through the yellow pine boards painted a grayish, off-white color.

Donald had enjoyed Bobbie's challenge to Milton's special privileges. He was small, without physical strength and unattractive. Milton had easily taken the Younger's affection away from him. Donald was darker complected and had pimples on his face that were a shade lighter than his skin. He was shy and seldom took part willingly in family affairs. His company wasn't enjoyable, while Milton was the outgoing, personable type which pleased the Younger's considerably.

Donald waited until Mrs. Younger had returned to the kitchen, before he tiptoed to Bobbie's room. He tapped with his knuckles, then whispered, "It's me, Donald." He walked in without getting a reply. Bobbie was on the bed with his hands clasped behind his head, his legs crossed defiantly. Donald sat on the edge of the bed and looked at Bobbie. He leaned closer. "Ain't she a bitch?"

The bathroom incident set the pattern for Bobbie's entire stay in the Younger house. He and Mrs. Younger became gradually more hostile towards each other. With Milton, it became pure hatred. With Mr. Younger, the indifference grew slowly into dislike. With Donald, it became friendship out of necessity. They both needed each other against Milton.

Donald served another need for Bobbie. He was easily dominated, and willingly became Bobbie's lackey. Bobbie cemented Donald's obedience during November.

Bobbie and Donald were walking to school. It was a chilly November day, and the smell of decaying leaves blended with the morning's misty residue left from a three-day storm. It was hard to breathe; like being in a steam bath, only chillier. Bobbie realized he needed an ally and saw it in Donald. He looked at Donald through the mist and asked. "Don't like Mrs. Younger, do ya? Milton, neither?"

"No! Can't stand 'em!" Donald answered. "That Milton makes me feel like a bug. The way he looks at me . . . talks down his nose at me." The hate in Donald's bulging black eyes was evident. His voice squeeked.

"Yeah, I know. Like t' punch him in his big nose!" Bobbie said with pleasure, realizing he would never try it. Milton was just too big! But he enjoyed the thought anyway. Bobbie returned to the business at hand. "I likes ya, Donald. . . . I know ya likes me. Let's fix that Milton. . . . What ya say?"

"I'm with you!" Donald stopped and looked at Bobbie. They both grinned and shook hands over the friendship pact, deciding to meet secretly in Bobbie's room that night.

The first meeting set the pattern. All meetings were held in Bobbie's room with Bobbie gradually taking command of their harassing campaign; designed to make life as miserable as possible for Milton, who was both neat and careful in dress and habits. They misplaced articles of clothing, wrinkled his ties and shirts, hid his shoes, tie clips, cuff links and anything else that was easily portable. Their timing and spacing was effective. Milton could never catch them, even though he was suspicious. With the hatred becoming more open, the tension was increasing between Bobbie and Milton and the breaking point was near.

Despite the friction in the foster home, Bobbie made a fairly good adjustment in his new school situation. He kept out of trouble while making fair scholastic progress. His successful experiences in the classroom at Hainesburg had tempered his general dislike of teachers and school work from open arrogance and sullen obedience to quiet conformity without hostility. Bobbie no longer answered his teachers back, slept in class or teased his classmates.

CHAPTER 17

Bobbie had forgotten about his parole obligation: the monthly visit to see his parole officer. Mrs. Younger reminded him on Sunday, November 8th, that Monday, the 9th, his month was up.

He took Monday off from school, and Mr. Younger volunteered to drive him into town, since it was on his way to work. It meant that he had to get the bus back which also gave him a chance to locate Rayford's address. Bobbie said to himself, when he walked out of the house that morning, "Shouldn't be too long, then I'll find Rayford's place." He reached inside his pocket, making sure he didn't forget Rayford's letter. Bobbie touched the paper envelope and smiled.

During the ride, Bobbie sat quietly, thinking about the explanations to use for Mrs. Younger's questions when he did get home. He interrupted his thoughts occasionally to answer a question by Mr. Younger. Bobbie made his choice just as Mr. Younger pulled over to the curb and stopped the car. "There you are, Bobbie," Mr. Younger said, pointing with his right index finger at the parole office building.

Surprised, momentarily, Bobbie's reflexes responded slowly but finally, he opened the door, stepped out of the car and stood on the sidewalk. He leaned over and said, "Thanks, Mr. Younger," and slammed the door shut.

Mr. Younger acknowledged the thank you with a nod, a half-wave and pulled out into traffic, leaving Bobbie staring at the building, sidewalk and the people hurrying to work.

Due at 9:00 a.m., Bobbie was five minutes early when he entered the gray, three story, concrete building and gave his name to the receptionist. It was ten minutes before he was directed to a second floor office, containing a wide, box-like desk, ready for work with a new green blotter and a wide, natural grain finish, oakwood chair with curving arms and spokes. Bobbie sat in an uncomfortable straight-backed, brown maple chair in front of the large overbearing desk, reflecting again that his explanation for Mrs. Younger would be good enough. He decided to himself, "Tell her I took a wrong bus back. Ended up on the other side of town. Had t' come all the way back. She'll swallow that one. Not that smart."

The last thought had hardly faded, when a door opened suddenly; a huge hulk flew past Bobbie, planting itself forcefully behind the desk. It stared out of large, oval-shaped, hazel eyes. When the huge head spoke, deep, resonant sounds vibrated through and past Bobbie, echoing off the ivory-white masonry walls.

"You're Bobbie Lee, right?" Mr. Harte asked, his baritone voice leaving little room for doubt.

"Yes," Bobbie answered; evaluating his opponent, while observing his red hair, red eyebrows, a long nose that curved to the right and his wide freckled face.

"I'm Mr. Harte. I'm the man you'll report to every month. You were on time. . . . I like that. My boys soon find out I don't put up with lateness!" He looked at Bobbie, arched his red eyebrows into two semicircles, then predicted; "We're going to get along all right."

Deciding that this was no man to fool around with, Bobbie said to himself, "Man, better play it straight with this guy!"

130

Bobbie was snapped out of his thoughts by loud, blunt questioning. Mr. Harte fired the questions at him in sequence, "Getting along all right in the Younger home? Anybody you don't like? What's happened, so far?"

Bobbie told him about the bathroom incident, and admitted he disliked Mrs. Younger and Milton Green. He didn't hold anything back, deciding to tell whatever he could remember. It came out in a torrent of words. He felt relieved, having told everything. The kind of relief one feels when he can start fresh, having gotten rid of excess baggage.

Michael Harte was a professional listener, attentively digesting the words, while studying Bobbie. He evaluated content and source; arriving at a conclusion, before Bobbie was finished. He now had a good idea of the living pattern in the Younger home. When Bobbie stopped talking, he leaned back in the chair, quietly relieved and slightly out of breath. Mr. Harte began the second round of questions and asked about school, friends and recreation.

Bobbie answered, "School's been okay. Ain't had no trouble with teachers. No fights with kids. Ain't the smartest. My teachers say I'm trying." He said to himself, "That's more'n my grammar school teachers use t' say." Bobbie continued talking about his lack of friends and recreation. He only had Donald Jacks as a friend and he was hardly any fun. While he was talking, unhappy flashes of memory focused rudely across his brain. Bobbie stopped talking, concentrating on the formerly forgotten incidents. He let Mr. Harte pick up the conversation, and carry it for awhile.

It was fifth grade. Bobbie was reading with his group in front of the class. They were spread out in a half circle. Mrs. Reaves had called on him to read and he stumbled over the words, mispronouncing every one. He remembered her lined face with its irritated look, the pursed lips and the strands of gray hair, hanging at her temples, when she ridiculed him in front of the group. "Bobbie Lee, you've been reading that story for a week! It's about time you started paying attention! Can't you remember any of the words?" It was the way she said it— the disgusted tone in her voice—that made him mad. He remembered answering her back; "If'n ya knew how t' teach, maybe I'd learn how t' read!" That was all she needed to hear. Bobbie was ordered to report to the principal's office.

The principal's office flashed into focus: the annoyed look on Mr. Mathews' face; the change to anger and the slap across his face, when he told Mr. Mathews what he thought of him and Mrs. Reaves. He recalled the sting vividly, it felt like pins sticking in his face, and still remembered the taste of salty tears dripping down his face.

Mr. Harte brought Bobbie back with pointed questioning. "Do you like Mr. Younger? Spend much time with you? Take you places?" Michael Harte always asked his questions in groups of three.

"He's all right, I guess. Ain't tough. Guess he's scared of Mrs. Younger." Bobbie paused to think about what he had just said. He decided to say something nice, even if he didn't really like the man. "Does offer t' take me an' the other boys places, like football games an' movies." After a pause, he added, "Ain't too bad. Guess he's all right."

It was ten minutes past 10:00 a.m., when Bobbie stepped out of the parole office building and the bright autumn sunshine made him squint. He walked mechanically, the required four city blocks to the bus stop; past the decorated store windows offering the latest autumn and back-to-school fashions. Bobbie didn't notice the gay, colorful displays; shirts and sweaters surrounded by autumn foliage and college football pennants. He was busy thinking about locating Rayford's address. Bobbie knew Rayford wouldn't be home now, but he wanted to leave a message. Let him know, he was back.

The bus ride was short, a little more than ten minutes to get to Pierson Street and North Fenton Avenue. Bobbie peered through the large glass window of the corner luncheonette; not seeing Rayford, he walked down the uneven, red brick sidewalk, checking the numbers over the doorways.

Rayford's house was at the end of the long, one-block street, about five hundred yards from North Fenton Avenue. It was an old, red brick, row house in poor condition. Mortar was missing between bricks, and there was a lightning-shaped crack down the middle of the house. The windows were unpainted, without storm sash, exposed to the full blunt of wind, rain and sun.

Bobbie walked up the worn stone steps and knocked on the dirty door covered with a coat of faded, peeling green paint. He had to knock three more times, before an elderly, white-haired, Negro woman opened the door about an inch and asked, "What you want, boy?"

"Rayford home?" Bobbie asked.

"No!" she answered, without opening the door any further.

"When's he comin' home?"

"After five. What you want him fo'?" She demanded in a peeved, raspy voice.

"I'm his friend, Bobbie Lee. Tell him I was here. Be seein' him, soon!"

"What's yo' name?"

"Bobbie Lee! I'm Rayford's friend!" Bobbie shouted for emphasis through the one-inch opening, hoping to impress his name on her hearing. "Tell him I was here. Be back soon!"

"All right, all right, I'll tell him!" She slammed the door in Bobbie's face, leaving him on the porch, staring at the door.

Bobbie didn't return to the Younger home until noon. Mrs. Younger was seated at the kitchen table having lunch. He greeted Mrs. Younger, sat down and waited for the questions. They came as expected, when she finished serving him a ham and cheese sandwich and a glass of milk.

Bobbie guessed right. His excuse about taking the wrong bus eased her suspicions. Bobbie handled Mrs. Younger smoothly, returned to school that afternoon and spent most of the day making plans. He wanted to get back with Rayford—soon. Bobbie liked being with Rayford. He didn't have to worry about doing anything wrong. With Rayford, everything was right.

CHAPTER 18

Bobbie faked a trip to the movies the following Saturday after his first trip in town, and was heading towards Mercerton by 1:00 p.m. He figured Rayford would be hanging around the corner luncheonette on a Saturday afternoon.

Bobbie figured right. He saw Rayford standing on the corner at North Fenton Avenue and Pierson Street. The bus had barely stopped, when Bobbie hopped off. Armed with a broad smile and a happy swagger, he approached Rayford. "Hi, Rayford!"

The voice, the small frame and the familiar face registered; Rayford smiled. "Hi, Bobbie!" Rayford extended his big, paw-like hand. He all but crushed Bobbie's miniature hand. "When ya get out?"

"Over a month ago. First chance I had t' come 'round was las' Monday. Did yo' mother tell ya?"

"Oh, yeah! . . . That was my grandmother. She said somebody was around. Couldn't remember who."

"Thought she was too ol' t' be yo' mother."

"Say, Bobbie, want ya t' meet a couple my buddies." Rayford pointed to the medium-sized, Negro youth next to him. "This here is Lenny."

"Hi, Lenny!" Bobbie looked at Lenny's heart-shaped blank face and waited.

"Hi," Lenny said without offering his hand. He kept both hands in his pockets and stared at Bobbie. Lenny had a big round head, thick kinky hair and a widow's peak in the middle of his forehead. He seldom smiled. With his long, flat-nosed face, Lenny would stare at people with dull black eyes and blank expression until it became annoying. Few people cared for his company.

"Hey, Shorty, com'ere!" Rayford hollered to a short, stocky, Negro youth sitting on a stone porch nearby. "Shorty meet Bobbie." After a pause, Rayford added, "Bobbie's a tough little stud!"

"Hi, Bobbie," Shorty said, offering his right hand, which helped relax Bobbie, who was hoping for a quick acceptance.

Rayford helped by keeping the conversation active. "You guys remember me tellin' about Bobbie." He looked at Lenny and Shorty.

"Yeah, I remember," Shorty replied and looked at Lenny. "You remember, don't ya Lenny?" His full, broad-featured face demanded a reply and his black eyes flashed a reminder.

"Yeah. . . . I remember," Lenny answered, staring at Bobbie.

Bobbie and Rayford spent the rest of the afternoon talking about Hainesburg, and their present home situations, while drinking coffee and eating sandwiches in the dirty but comfortable "greasy spoon" that was passing for a luncheonette. Their stomachs full, they decided to leave and locate Bobbie's address, figuring it would be easier to get Bobbie than waiting until he got in town. They drove out to the township in Shorty's decrepit sedan, riding on four bald tires. In the car, the feelings were mixed; Rayford and Bobbie were talking and laughing, while Shorty and Lenny were quiet. When Rayford said Bobbie was going to be part of the gang, Shorty agreed with a nod of his head and was surprised at Rayford's excited voice. Lenny was quiet and only answered when

136

questioned. He didn't volunteer any enthusiasm when Bobbie was included in their schemes.

Bobbie decided that since Rayford was the leader it didn't matter what the others thought. He gave directions, relaxed and enjoyed the ride. They turned into Lawnside Avenue and cruised slowly, marking mentally the landmarks; especially Bobbie's house.

After checking the area, Rayford instructed Shorty to turn at the first corner and drive around the block; back to their original entry on Lawnside Avenue. They pulled off the Laurelton Road, parked on the shoulder and held an impromptu meeting in the car.

The date was set for Monday. They would meet Bobbie on the corner of Lawnside Avenue and Laurelton Road at 11:00 p.m. Rayford planned to get some "fast" money and was going to show Bobbie how to do it, modern style, by auto.

Monday night, Bobbie went upstairs promptly at nine, undressed and went through the usual toilet ritual before retiring. He lay under the warm woolen blanket in the dark, listening and waiting. He heard Donald climb the stairs, then splashing sounds, footsteps, a door shutting and again—quiet. Donald was followed by Milton shortly afterwards. Bobbie listened to his sequence of muted sounds. He was waiting for the two key persons to retire. Their bedroom was downstairs in the back of the house, next to the kitchen. The Youngers were "day people," retiring nightly by ten. They didn't keep Bobbie waiting, by ten-thirty, he could hear Mr. Younger snoring. Bobbie laughed to himself. He pictured Mr. Younger downstairs with his mouth open, "blowin' zeeze" as Rayford would say.

Bobbie quietly opened the window, a little at a time, and slipped his narrow frame out to the porch roof. The asphalt shingles provided a silent surface. He was glad that it was shingle, instead of noisy tin. Bobbie slid down the wood support pillar with his legs and arms wrapped around the post like a monkey. On the porch, Bobbie stood still, listening to the night sounds. It was a full minute before he moved again. He was roadside by 11:00 p.m., waiting promptly for Shorty's car, which could be recognized easily by its rattling and squeaking.

The timing was accurate that night. Bobbie had to wait a short five minutes. By eleven-thirty, they were riding through the narrow dark streets in the northern section of Mercerton, searching for prospects.

As for their methods, it would be hit and run supported by pipes, hard rubber hoses, a blackjack and a stocking containing a lead ball. It was crude and makeshift but effective.

Rayford set the mood for the night exclaiming, "Bobbie, you're gonna see some action t'night! Gonna show ya how t' make a quick buck." Laughing, he nudged Lenny, "Ain't that right, Lenny?"

"Yeah, man, jus' watch us t'night!" Lenny answered.

They spotted the "ripe" prospect, before he turned into the side street as they came down Carlyle Avenue. After slowing down to check Carlyle Avenue both directions, they shot down the side street and pulled over to the curb. The whale-like, modern steel chariot belched two agile shadows, swinging their deadly weapons in the night air. Rayford kept banging away with the blackjack, while Lenny swung the lead-filled stocking. The stunned, battered victim slumped heavily to the concrete, bleeding from severe head wounds. The two shadows rifled through the victim's clothing, removing the wallet, wrist watch and pocket change without listening to the pitiful moans.

138

Bobbie watched Rayford and Lenny from inside the car. He enjoyed every second of it. Rayford and Lenny were good. They knew how to beat a victim to a bloody pulp in fifteen seconds.

Rayford liked his good times and didn't let work interfere with his pleasures. With the money from mugging jobs, they stored wine, whiskey, beer and cigarettes, with reefers for extra kicks in Shorty's car.

At fifteen, Bobbie became expert at smoking oval-shaped reefers as well as the regular round cigarettes. And his young body was used to the new liquid diet of cheap brands of wine, whiskey and beer. But he still had one big pleasure to sample—sex.

Two weeks after his first lesson in violent crime, Bobbie got in the car expecting the usual group, but was surprised to see a woman sitting in the back between Rayford and Lenny. She was drinking from a bottle of wine and rubbing Rayford's leg, while Lenny was caressing her exposed breast. Rayford introduced Bobbie, after she finished drinking. "Bobbie, this here is Maybelline." Rayford pointed to the dark-skinned, middle-aged woman with frizzled hair, broad features and pronounced lips that were opened in a moist smile.

"Hi," Bobbie said, then looked at Rayford.

Maybelline leaned forward and squinted. She reached out and pinched Bobbie's cheek, lisping, "You're a cute little stud." Bobbie became warm and embarrassed, but let her pinch and pat his face, listening to her baritone, hoarse voice and lisping speech. "Still got a cherry?" She leaned back and asked Rayford, "Bobbie got a cherry?"

"Yeah," Rayford said with a broad, toothy grin.

Maybelline returned to Bobbie. "Gonna get it, Bobbie!" she laughed. Annoyed, she turned to Lenny and blurted out, "Stop suckin' on me!" She pushed Lenny away and took another swig of wine, making gulping sounds, while it dripped off her chin.

"Gonna be some night!" thought Bobbie, as he leaned back to get comfortable and enjoy the show.

The light from the airport beacon was flashing with monotonous regularity across the cool, clear, autumn night. Bobbie was standing with Lenny and Shorty near a clump of birch trees with thinning yellow leaves. They were waiting their "turns" on the dark side road near the county airport. It was rotation sex with seniority setting the order of turns. Rayford was first with Shorty getting "sloppy" seconds, Lenny "sweaty" thirds and Bobbie, as anchor man, "disgusting" fourths. It was sex served assembly line style in a filthy car, reeking an odorous blend; alcohol, sweat and sex.

It became Bobbie's turn, when Lenny's moving shadow stepped out of the larger, stationary shadow. Rayford slapped Bobbie on the back. "Go get it, Bobbie! Maybelline can really move!"

The car stunk. But Bobbie got used to it soon enough as he and the drunken, spread-eagled, sex machine united on the squeaky back seat. He could smell her body odor and wine breath, when she lisped in his ear, "Com'on, Bobbie, wail!" After three quick minutes, butting against the drunken Maybelline, Bobbie joined the club—he got his first piece. He was no longer the innocent adolescent. Rayford was developing his pupil into a permanent member of the gang entitled to all rights and privileges.

Rayford was understanding. He realized Bobbie couldn't get out too often. Bobbie didn't want to chance sneaking out of the house more than once, possibly twice a week, if he were needed for some mugging or car pilfering work. By keeping his night trips down to a weekly

140

minimum, he was able to keep from getting caught. Bobbie sensed that a certain amount of luck was involved. He didn't want to spoil a good thing.

Rayford taught Bobbie how to enter locked cars and "jump" ignition wires under dashboards. The gang liked to ride in new Cadillacs, Thunderbirds and Imperials. It was a "real ball," driving those big, beautiful, luxury cars around the city streets. They always returned them to the same parking spot, and the unsuspecting owners seldom noticed the slight decrease in the gas gauge.

Bobbie was also trained in the finer arts of crap shooting and cards. He learned all the little tricks that helps one win more often. The gang needed to win more often, they had heavy expenses; whiskey, cigarettes, reefers and presents for their women. Maybelline would do on occasion, but they preferred variety, especially younger, more attractive girls.

Life was becoming a series of new thrills for Bobbie. After a swinging night of alcohol and reefers, Bobbie came home walking on his toes. He laughed to himself as he climbed the front porch pillar, "Man, 'nother reefer, I'd fly up on the roof!"

It was a "ball" with Rayford compared to the dull routine with the Youngers. Bobbie enjoyed the exciting secret feeling. No one in the house suspected anything— not even Donald. Bobbie kept his escapades a complete secret. They were his to be enjoyed, alone.

CHAPTER 19

When autumn's oranges and reds faded to dull brown and winter's white covered the ground, Rayford's gang operations slowed to a frozen crawl.

The frequent, deep snows formed an impasse to the suburbs, keeping Bobbie isolated from them through most of January and February. But with March, came an early thaw. The melting snow signaled the return to their aggressive activities.

But Bobbie was thinking about more than just the usual pattern of violent crime. He saw a chance for revenge against a past enemy, Joe Wilson. He remembered his vow to get him, and decided to take advantage of Rayford's gang. Bobbie knew he couldn't revenge his mother's death alone. Joe Wilson was a brutal animal, who would enjoy clobbering him again, if he were foolish enough to attempt it alone.

It was a typical April night. The day's showers ended in the afternoon, and left a cool nip in the air that made a sweater feel comfortable and physical exercise a pleasure—a perfect night to see an old friend again.

They cruised Bobbie's old neighborhood, following his directions. Bobbie still remembered Joe's old haunts. They were going to combine business with pleasure; Bobbie's pleasure, Rayford's business.

Bobbie spotted Joe Wilson talking to a companion at the corner of Morrow and Hall Streets. He told Shorty to park on Hall Street a half-block down from the corner near Alliance Street. Bobbie recalled that Joe lived on Alliance near Merchant, and would have to walk past them to get home. They waited patiently, smoking cigarettes and gulping wine. Bobbie didn't drink that night. He just sat quietly, thinking about Joe Wilson and fingered the blackjack in his hand. It was going to feel good, smashing Joe Wilson's face to a bloody mess.

Joe Wilson bellowed a hoarse, drunken good-bye to his friend, and started wobbling down Hall Street. Lenny was the first to see him approach. "He's comin'!" he warned the others. The close atmosphere of alcohol and cigarette smoke suddenly became tense, business-like. Rayford nodded to Bobbie. He was allowing him to take command.

Bobbie loved it; being the leader. He became serious and intent, with all the concentration he could muster. He almost barked out the orders but gained control of himself. With a slight quiver in his voice, he said to Rayford and Lenny, "Jump out the car, soon's he's pas'. Grab him from behind. Won't know what's happenin'. If he breaks yo' grip, hit him. But save the las' fo' me. When ya got him, I'll jump out."

"Might remember ya," Rayford said.

"Don't give a shit!"

Rayford laughed.

Bobbie said, "After I club the shit outta him, check his pockets."

"Got money on him?" Rayford asked.

"Yeah," Bobbie replied. "Likes t' carry lotsa money." Bobbie paused, then added, 'Likes t' show off in bars. . . . Thinks he's big shit!"

They lapsed into silence; the silent, tense waiting of the hunt. Only this hunt was slightly different. The prey was human.

143

Joe Wilson hardly noticed the parked car. He was drunk and feeling no pain; unaware of the shadows waiting inside the car. The location was excellent. The nearest street light was back at Morrow and Hall Streets with all the stores and houses locked for the night. When Joe Wilson stumbled past the car, the shadows suddenly became real. He heard the doors opening, heard the steps towards him, then felt a heavy blow on his head. Unable to break the grip of the thick, strong arms around his neck, he lisped, "What's a matter wish ya! Lemme go! Ya sonna bish!"

Those were the last words Joe Wilson said that night. Bobbie hurried around the front of the car and was in front of the startled drunk. Rayford and Lenny had his arms pinned behind him, and Bobbie started hitting him in the face with the blackjack.

"If it ain't the great Joe Wilson!" Bobbie let the words dribble out of the side of his mouth, then he swung with all his strength and cracked the blackjack across the confused face. They heard the crunching cheek bones, and watched Joe Wilson bite in pain against the dirty, stained rag, serving as a bit. "This one's fo' her," Bobbie said to himself, and swung again; the swinging force lifted him off his heels.

The throbbing pain was too much for Joe Wilson. He tried to break the grip and get at the small, unfamiliar object causing all the unbearable pain. His whiskey soaked brain couldn't recognize the face in the dark.

Bobbie gave no quarter, whacking Joe Wilson five more times over his head and face. After the last swing, he stopped. Exhausted, he examined the results. Joe Wilson's chin was resting against his chest. He was barely conscious. They let him crumble to the littered, grimy sidewalk, then Bobbie kicked him in the stomach for good measure. He moaned. His head fell loosely against the concrete. Then it was quiet . . . but only for a few seconds.

Rayford and Lenny stripped his pockets of thirty-two dollars, assorted change, his gold watch and gold ring for a complete haul. It was a profitable night; money, jewelry and revenge, tinted with sadistic pleasure. They were a content group driving back to Laurelton Township. Bobbie wanted to make sure he got home early enough to get up for school. He had faked being sick the last time out.

"Man, what a haul!" Rayford shouted over the noisy engine. Shorty's car had been getting worse. It was about ready for the junkyard.

Usually silent, Lenny exclaimed, "Gonna get me new shoes!" Everybody laughed on that one.

"When we gonna split?" Shorty asked. Shorty always was practical. He never felt satisfied, until he had the money in his pocket.

"We can split the money now. Sell the ring an' watch later. Okay?" Rayford asked, trying to satisfy everybody.

"Don't want no money. You guys split it," Bobbie said. He didn't want any of Joe Wilson's money. The revenge was enough. Bobbie wanted to forget all about Joe Wilson, after he read tomorrow's newspapers. He was sure it would make it. Violence was a good news item. "After the papers," he thought, "I'll fo'get that no-good, mother-humper ever lived!"

"Don't want none?" Rayford asked. He looked at Bobbie but couldn't see his features in the dark.

"Yeah." Bobbie laughed and looked at Lenny. "Lenny'll have mo' fo' shoes."

Lenny reached over and squeezed Bobbie's shoulder. It was the first sign of acceptance by Lenny, since Bobbie became part of the group. Lenny said, "You're okay, Bobbie." Lenny's gesture added to Bobbie's successful night.

Bobbie read the report in the evening newspaper the following night, thoroughly. He had only read the larger type above the column on the morning papers. He didn't want to make Donald curious or suspicious, when they stopped at the candy store on the way to school. Bobbie enjoyed the details in the article about Joe Wilson and his condition in the hospital. They expected him to need plastic surgery, and he was unable to give an accurate description or identify his assailants. Bobbie didn't understand the meaning of plastic surgery, but guessed its connection with the face. He had hurt Joe Wilson severely and was satisfied. He was even now, yet safe. Joe Wilson never knew what hit him or who did it. Closing the paper, Bobbie said to himself, "Now I can fo'get 'bout him." He dropped the newspaper on the floor, climbed the stairs and went to bed; not bothering to wash or brush his teeth. He was too tired to care. Sleep came easily. Within five minutes, he was breathing deep, rhythmic breaths. It was going to be a rewarding night's sleep. The best in a long time.

CHAPTER 20

It had to happen—and it did happen—exactly one year to the day, after Bobbie's placement in the Younger home.

Bobbie and Milton shared mutual feelings of pure, simple hatred. And Bobbie's subtle, harassing pranks had finally reached the breaking point. Milton declared that same night: "If that Bobbie Lee plays another trick on me, I'm gonna lay my fists all over his face!"

This was one of those rare occasions, when Bobbie stretched his luck and obliged Milton by pouring vinegar into his after shave lotion. Bobbie knew Milton was proud of the fact that he was a steady shaver, and liked to splash a lot of perfumed lotion on his face.

Milton was in a hurry and shaved right after supper. When the usually refreshing lotion, now spiked with potent cider vinegar, made contact with Milton's tender skin, he winced in pain. That was it! With his face still stinging, he ran downstairs shouting, "Bobbie Lee, I'm gonna beat your black ass!"

Mrs. Younger was shocked at Milton's descriptive language, and rose to the occasion like a formidable knight-on-horse. "Milton, stop that kind of talk! I won't have it in my house!"

Running past Mrs. Younger, as if she were invisible, Milton didn't stop until he was outside grappling with Bobbie. He caught Bobbie by surprise, grabbing him by the throat with his left hand and with his right hand, slapped him three times in sucsession.

With his face smarting and Milton's hand squeezing his throat, Bobbie kicked Milton in his left shin bone. The pain raced up Milton's left leg, registering on his brain with throbbing impact. Milton used both hands to rub his leg, leaving his defenses open. Bobbie saw his chance and brought his left knee hard against Milton's chest, knocking him on his back. Then, he ran to the side of the garage and picked up a surplus fence slat. He approached Milton, who was crouched on the grass, taking deep gulps of air. "Get up, an' I'll split yo' head!" Bobbie stated with clipped speech, quivering voice.

Milton didn't answer. He kept gasping for air. But Mrs. Younger, now part of the scene, helped Milton get up. She looked back over her shoulder, while helping Milton walk towards the house and said to Bobbie, "You're not going to be in this house long." Spitting the last words out, she said, "You little criminal!"

Bobbie just stood there, holding the board; a chain of thoughts racing through his head:

"I goofed! Now she's gonna kick me out! Mr. Messner'll tell Mr. Harte. He'll send me back t' Hainesburg . . . ain't goin' back . . . even if I gotta run away. . . . Yeah . . . run away!"

The idea about running away occupied his mind for the rest of the evening, while he wandered the streets in the immediate neighborhood. He had walked away from the house, declining to face Mrs. Younger's wrath. With his hands forced into his pockets, his head tilted downward and a frown on his face, he kept thinking: "Got t' get away!" But he kept asking himself, "How?" Then the idea dawned on him. "Mr. Younger's car! Yeah . . . he'll be home by ten. Steal his car an' get Rayford. We'll get out of town fas'!" He walked another block, then said out loud, "Gonna do it t'night!" For emphasis he added, "Really mean it! Gonna do it t'night! . . . Gotta do it . . . t'night!"

Having convinced himself that it was the only way to keep from returning to Hainesburg, he dragged himself back allowing enough time for nightfall and Mr. Younger to bring home "his" car.

With Mrs. Younger's tongue lashing still ringing in his ears, Bobbie sat by the window listening patiently to the night breezes chasing the dry brown leaves. The night was black with thick overcast clouds, blocking out a full moon and a sky full of stars.

Carrying a small, overnight bag with a comb, tooth-brush and change of underwear, and wearing a light-weight jacket, Bobbie climbed out of his bedroom window for the last time. He held the bag handle in his teeth, slid down the wood pillar to the porch, then walked silently around the house towards the garage. The old sagging garage doors opened willingly, but the eerie creaking from the rusty hinges startled Bobbie. He looked toward the house, wondering if they heard the creaking sounds, amplified by the night's sudden stillness.

Bobbie found a flashlight in the glove compartment which helped him locate the ignition wires to cross breed the electrical current. The motor responded to the unusual starting procedure on the first try with a loud explosion, then settled down to a steady idle. Bobbie used the flashlight to locate the headlights, dashboard lights and put the automatic gear shift into reverse position. He was glad that Mr. Younger had shown him how to operate the car during the get-acquainted-period, and that Shorty had given him an occasional driving lesson in the old junk.

There was one glaring flaw in Bobbie's driving ability, he never learned to drive in reverse. It took him longer than expected to navigate the driveway. Narrowly missing the side of the garage, he corrected his direction and almost crashed into the rear porch. Bobbie had to locate the drive position, drive forward and then try reverse again. He started backing up again but in the opposite direction, ending his second attempt on the lawn, crushing Mrs. Younger's favorite shrubbery. Correcting again, he maneuvered onto the driveway, narrowly missing the house. But he did scrape the rear right fender against the left side of the front porch.

It seemed like almost an hour, before Bobbie could get the gear shift back into drive and head forward; the wrong way up the narrow, one-way street.

Unaware of anyone watching his progress, he shot forward with tires screeching, engine roaring, expelling a trail of oil smoke and burning rubber.

Mr. Younger, in his maroon housecoat, looked at his wife. "He's taking my car!" he said to her as if he believed she could do something about it.

Mrs. Younger, also in a maroon housecoat, gave an extra tug to her belt, adjusted her collar and declared for action; "We'll call the police. That little car thief won't get far!" She led her husband back into the house heading straight for the telephone. While Mrs. Younger was dialing, she had to wave down Donald and Milton with promises to explain after the call. Mr. Younger attempted to end their questions and said, "He took my car!" From the tone in his voice, he still couldn't believe it.

Bobbie's driving was erratic. He left some blue paint on a yellow convertible parked on narrow Lawnside Avenue. Despite the minor scraping, he kept going and managed to drive the entire length of Laurelton Road without crashing into anything. But it was at the Carlyle Circle that he ran into trouble.

Bobbie was doing close to sixty when he came to the sharply curving circle. He tried to slow down but couldn't. The circle zoomed up in front of him, before he could turn the wheel. The car swerved out of control, bumping over the curb, making two loud thumping thuds. Bobbie was jarred against the roof, his hands releasing control of the steering wheel. The car's momentum propelled it into a thick oak tree, followed by the sickening, crashing sounds of breaking glass and bending steel. Bobbie's ill-fated trip was over in three short miles. With his bruised head resting against the window, he listened to the sound of hissing steam escaping from the cracked radiator. Then his head fell against the steering wheel.

CHAPTER 21

Bobbie had been in a bewildered state, since the accident. He regained a hazy consciousness the first week in the hospital, and was hardly aware of the antiseptic odor and constant traffic in his ten-bed ward for the remainder of the second week.

From the hospital, Bobbie was taken to the Youth House to await his trial. Two weeks passed before they held the trial—Bobbie's second time around the juvenile court circuit. It was completed without him—in a sense. He was withdrawn, answering the judge's questions in one or two words, never volunteering any information or lifting his head to look at the judge. He didn't move or lift his eyes off the long dark wood table, when the judge sentenced him to Farmdale rather than Hainesburg. Bobbie was deep inside his shell, sitting quietly before the judge. He barely listened to the logical reasons for being sent to Farmdale; something about a need for stricter supervision. Bobbie didn't really care why.

By nine the next morning, Bobbie was on his way to Farmdale. He sat in the rear seat with two other boys, but refused to talk to them. They shrugged Bobbie's refusal off, keeping up a lively chatter between themselves. Bobbie wasn't in the mood for any small talk. He just wanted to sit and think about the past month and put the pieces together, before he got to Farmdale. He stared out the window on his side but didn't see any details, just one big blur. His eyes were on himself, reliving the accident, the two weeks in the hospital, the two uneventful weeks in the Youth House and then the trial.

With the past four weeks locked in place, Bobbie was now ready to think about the present. The questions skipped through his mind:

"Where I'm goin' now? . . . Farmdale? . . . Where's Farmdale? . . . Heard 'bout it in Hainesburg. . . . Can't remember how far. . . . Ever gonna see Rayford again? . . . The judge say a year? . . . Yeah. . . . A whole year!"

Busy with his thoughts, Bobbie saw little of the changing countryside. They kept in a northerly direction, and the gently rolling farmland gradually raised into the foothills of the Appalachian Mountains. The autumn scene was alive with color; yellow birches, yellow-red maples, crimson oaks and the acrid, nostalgic smell of burning leaves, filling the air. It was nature at its best; streaks and splashes of color across the hills, beckoning beauty seekers and challenging aspiring artists to recapture its beauty with vibrant brush strokes. This vista of color was wasted on Bobbie, whose eyes were turned inward.

Bobbie entered Farmdale with mild curiosity, and suffered quietly through its brief orientation program. He did very little talking and didn't make any new friends, hoping to settle down to a routine life, without attracting any attention. Bobbie wanted to.be left alone, put in his time and get out. But his cottage mates resented his silence, even the guards resented it. They wouldn't leave him alone, and kept trying to draw him out of his shell.

Even Bobbie noticed gradually how different Farmdale was from Hainesburg, which had the college campus atmosphere combined with the gentle philosophy to understand and help boys; while Farmdale was a state farm with uniformed guards to enforce its rules, without a lenient, helpful philosophy or purpose.

153

Bobbie managed to avoid making close friends or enemies with his cottage mates or with his workmates on farm-duty chores. He enjoyed the farm work. It helped pass the dreary days, which he marked off on a small, pocket-sized calendar. But there was one flaw in his otherwise uneventful career at Farmdale.

Of all the guards who came in contact with Bobbie, there was one who disliked him so much, it bordered on the edge of pure hatred. It was one of those hard to explain clashes of personality. Bobbie didn't have to do or say anything. Vic McShea just didn't like him.

Their first meeting on the first day set the pattern for the entire year at Farmdale.

It was after supper and they were being marched back to their cottage. Bobbie kept falling out of cadence and was indifferent to the whole thing. "Hey you!. . . Shorty!. . . Yeah, you!" Vic McShea blasted out, becoming angry. His neck getting redder with every word. "Get in step, before I yank ya outta there!"

Bobbie didn't know he was making an enemy of the notorious guard known as Big Vic, who was the most feared, therefore the most respected guard. He was addressed as Mr. McShea, by everyone, including the other guards. His six-six, bear-like frame of bone and muscle scared you into respecting him. He had thick arms, wide shoulders, and hands like two hams which made even the toughest inmates think twice before talking back. He combed his straight blond hair over his forehead, covering a battle scar. But it only added to the mean, scowling expression. His face, with its broken, squat nose, seldom revealed his true feelings but he was one of the few guards that was really happy in his job. He loved to push the "punks" around.

McShea's nickname for Bobbie was "Eight Ball," and

he used it often. He never called him Bobbie or Lee. He would just blast out an order: "Hey, Eight Ball! Get your skinny little ass over here!"

Bobby would seethe inside, shuffle over and wait for the order rigid as a robot. "Go help clean out the shithouse. Don't let me catch ya goofin' off. Ya hear?"

Bobbie would pick up his head, nod and shuffle away, his head shifting loosely from side to side, while rolling his eyes in quiet defiance.

It was hardly more than two months after his arrival, that Bobbie rolled his eyes a little too quickly and McShea's alert gray eyes caught him doing it. He lifted Bobbie up with one hand, choking the air out of his throat. At eye level, Bobbie's feet dangled like a dummy's. McShea stared at Bobbie's tortured face. "Gonna roll your eyes at me again?" Bobbie couldn't answer. He could only dangle at the mercy of the ugly giant.

The second time McShea caught Bobbie rolling his eyes at him, he lifted Bobbie off the floor and sent him flying across the long cottage room. Bobbie ended his unscheduled flight in an unconscious heap under an overturned bunk. Before he tossed Bobbie like a toy, McShea shouted across the room, "No skinny, eight ball nigger's gonna get wise wid me!" Bobbie decided to stop rolling his eyes at Vic McShea, and switched to more practical, crafty methods.

It took over a week but Bobbie located Vic McShea's car at its secret parking place. McShea kept his car away from the cottage area, knowing how they felt about him. Bobbie's subtle tricks against McShea's car included long scratches across the beautiful red paint on the sleek convertible's sides and fenders, sudden flat tires and an overheated motor from a thirsty, drained out radiator.

McShea couldn't pick on Bobbie for his sudden car

troubles. Bobbie wasn't the only boy in the cottage being used as his private punching bag. There were thirty-five angry boys, just dreaming of ways to get back at him and he knew it. McShea was hated by white inmates as well as the colored. He accepted it without concern, enjoying his work too much to worry about what a few "punks" thought of him. But Bobbie did have one victory. McShea stopped bringing his car, riding instead with another guard.

McShea's severe discipline methods were known to the top staff members in Farmdale but he was efficient and kept the cottage under control. There was never any trouble at his cottage. His methods were overlooked in favor of the results, without concern for the effect on the inmates—a growing hatred of authority.

The effect on Bobbie was noticeable. He was beginning to hate Farmdale, almost as much as the Bear, Vic McShea's animal nickname. He said to another colored boy, while working in the packing shed, "Hates that ugly, white trash so much, got 'nough lef' over t' hate all white trash."

"Me too, Bobbie! Feels the same way!" His face tightened and squint lines formed around his eyes, then the other boy added, "Makes me sick to look at him. So mean and ugly lookin'!"

Once Bobbie realized he was different from white boys, he became suspicious of all white people. But as long as he stayed within his small, protective, "colored" world, he felt secure and kept his distance from white people and their world. In Farmdale, his dormant suspicions festered into an open sore. Bobbie's resentment gradually became open hatred. He was tired of being pushed around. He wanted to do some of the pushing.

"Jes wait'll I get off this asshole farm!" Bobbie said

to the room, while lying awake on his bunk in the cool darkness. He stopped breathing for a few seconds, listening to the heavy, regular breathing from the slumbering lumps in the other bunks. He spoke again, "Ain't gonna take no shit from nobody!" Someone stirred at the far end of the long room. Bobbie stopped, waited, then deciding to get some sleep, turned on his right side and spit out the words, "Go screw yo'selves, ev'rybody!" He pushed his head into the pillow and squeezed his eyes shut, trying to force sleep.

It was two days before Bobbie's release date, and Vic McShea and Leon Sparkman were enjoying a coffee break. Sparkman was one of the meeker guards, who let Vic McShea push him around.

Sparkman, who's face resembled a weasel, leaned forward as if to ferret for chicken eggs and said with a sly grin crossing his face, "Your boy gets out Friday."

"Who?"

"Your boy, Lee!"

"Oh, that little son-of-a-bitch!" Vic Shea gulped a long drink of coffee and wiped his chin with the back of his huge right hand. His chin wiped dry, the warm coffee working its way down, he looked at Sparkman and confessed with mild alarm, "Gee, almost forgot his time was up!"

"Yeah, year's up already."

"Say, only got two days to get my last licks in!"

McShea thought about the pleasure he got, slapping that little eight ball around. His face beamed a smile, showing all his yellow-stained teeth. He leaned toward Sparkman. "I'll see that little monkey tonight, after chow." McShea nudged Sparkman. "Pay my farewell respects." They both laughed, slurped their coffee and hand wiped their damp chins. They were a contented pair; the bear with his weasel companion.

At six, McShea walked into the cottage and headed straight for Bobbie's bunk. "Hey, boy!" McShea said at Bobbie. "Wanna talk private wid ya in the shower room."

Bobbie stayed at his bunk. The other boys nearby acted as if they were deaf, and kept busy with their personal chores.

"Did ya hear me, boy?" the voice getting angrier.

"I heard ya . . . Mr. McShea."

"G'wan, get movin'!" McShea barked.

Bobbie waited, draining every ounce out of the seconds, then started shuffling towards the shower room. He had a funny feeling in the pit of his stomach, this wasn't going to be a pleasant, friendly chat.

In the shower room, McShea got down to business right away. Bobbie alternated his cold, defiant stare from the large fist grasping his shirt to the large, moon-shaped face glaring down at him.

The face spoke; "Since you're gettin' out Friday, I'm remindin' ya not to try nothin' funny wid my car." McShea was bringing his car to work again. McShea twisted Bobbie's shirt, drawing it in tighter and choking him.

Bobbie gasped, "Don't have t' worry 'bout me."

"Not gonna try nothin'?"

"No."

"Okay . . . here's a sample of what you'll get, if ya decide to change your mind." He slapped Bobbie four times, using the palm and the back of his right hand. "Get me?" he asked, after he finished.

"Yeah. . . . I get ya," Bobbie answered with tears running down his cheeks, leaving a wet trail over the stinging pain. McShea let him go and he fell to the floor sobbing. Vic McShea stood over him and watched. His stern, rigid face broke into a wide smile.

158

When they drove off the state farm grounds, Bobbie breathed a sigh of relief and said to himself, "Finally got that big bastard off my back!"

Mr. James Finn, the caseworker who was now supervising Bobbie, had the chore of delivering him to the foster home. He heard the sigh, turned his head and asked, "Glad to get out?" He stared at Bobbie with deep-set, brown eyes.

"Sho is!" Bobbie answered, while looking at James Finn's long, curving nose.

"Want to tell me about Farmdale?"

"Not much t' tell . . . 'cept I didn't like the guards," Bobbie answered; hesitant to bare his soul.

"Treated you rough?" Mr. Finn asked, as he turned left, weaving into the traffic on the main, concrete highway, heading south towards Mercerton.

"Don't treat ya nice!"

Mr. Finn got the hint, Bobbie was not going to talk about Farmdale, so he changed his approach from past to present. "I'm taking you to a home in Adams Township."

"Mrs. Younger don't want me back?"

"Yes, that's about it." James Finn pursed his small mouth.

"Kinda figured that . . . after what I did." Bobbie looked at Mr. Finn's red-tinted brown hair that was beginning to gray at the temples.

"Don't worry about her, Bobbie, just try and stay out of trouble."

"Yeah," Bobbie said, "mo' trouble ya get in, worser places they put ya."

"You've got something there. Know what the worst place is . . . don't you?"

"Yeah, the prison!"

"Can't get any worst. Keep getting in trouble, you'll end up there. Take my advice. Be extra careful this time."

James Finn stopped talking and laughed to himself, "Here I go again, preaching." He thought for a minute, then decided to talk about the foster home and stop preaching. "It's better to get Bobbie mentally set for the placement," he said to himself. Then he said to Bobbie, "Do you know where Adams Township is?"

"Don't think so . . . Near Mercerton?"

"Yes, and the home's on Parkview Avenue near Adams High. You'll be going to the new junior high."

Bobbie was silent, staring through the window, thinking, "Maybe I ain't goin' back t' school. Seventeen now. Can quit, if'n I want to." Then he realized his situation, and the natural question arose in his mind: "Do I have t' get the state's permission?" He turned toward Mr. Finn and asked, "Do I gotta get the state's permission t' quit school?"

"Yes, Bobbie. We're your guardian. We give the permission for the state."

"Oh!" Bobbie said.

"We usually let our children quit school, if they'd be better off working."

"If'n I don't do good in school, better off quittin'."

"Have to see how you make out, before we make any plans," Mr. Finn replied.

The last half of the thirty-five mile trip was endured quietly by both parties. They looked at the autumn hues outlining the green dairy farm pastures and the rolling hills, flying past their speeding car.

When they arrived in Mercerton, Bobbie thought about his new foster home. It wasn't long, before he asked, "Far from town?"

"A couple miles," Mr. Finn answered.

Bobbie recorded the fact and estimated the distance to Rayford's home, then said to himself, "Rayford still 'round? Sho be glad t' see him 'gain!" Bobbie didn't want to think about not seeing Rayford again, so he pushed that unhappy thought out of his mind.

They turned off South Enterprise Street, drove past the high school and after three blocks, turned left on Parkview Avenue. Bobbie looked at the sparse landscaping, the single, frame houses and the dirt walks without curbing. He thought, "Not nice like Lawnside. . . . Still beats the farm!"

They parked in front of a two and one-half story, frame house covered with imitation stone facing. It was gaudy with too many pink and buff-colored stones. Bobbie noticed it was one of the older homes in the block, and compared it to the Younger home. He shrugged, stepped out of the car and said to himself, "It'll do fo' 'while."

Bobbie endured the introductions to the foster parents, a Mr. and Mrs. George Hill, inspected the room that he was going to share with another youth, Alvin Thomas, who was sixteen, and then toured the rest of the house. He didn't talk during the tour, except to answer a direct question. Bobbie was glad when it was over.

Mrs. Hill impressed Bobbie as a fairly nice person, and

he predicted he wouldn't have too much trouble with her. He decided, "Won't be a bitch like Mrs. Younger!" Mr. Hill didn't appear to be the mousy type. "Bet he don't take no shit off nobody!" Bobbie thought. "Ain't 'bout t' give him none! Biggest stud I ever seen! Bigger'n that bastard, McShea!"

He met the other youths as they filtered home one at a time. The four youths, Bobbie and the Hills, made a good-size family at the supper table that night. The boys' ages ranged from fourteen to eighteen and Bobbie's room-mate was the friendliest. He was glad that he was sharing Alvin's room. During supper, he watched the Hills and the other boys and before it was over, he decided, "Talk t' Alvin t'night. Get the scoop on things. Don't want no trouble, like I had at the Youngers."

Alvin was tall, lanky and awkward. He had happy black eyes that blended with his smile. His long brown face was an open invitation to be friends. Bobbie responded readily, welcoming the chance for a friendly, after-hours private chat.

Alvin sat on the large double bed, while Bobbie lounged in the cushioned rocking chair. They were both wrapped in blue robes, covering white shorts and tee shirts.

"Won't mind it too much around here, Bobbie," Alvin commented, while watching his big toes gyrate in restricted circles.

Bobbie watched Alvin's toes and laughed, revealing both rows of white teeth. Recovering, he questioned Alvin, "Make ya keep stric' hours?"

"Yeah. No late hours around here. No back talk, neither!"

"Can see that!" Bobbie declared. "Mr. Hill looks rough."

162

"He sure is! Straightened out Willie last week. . . . Say, what school you goin' to?" Alvin's forehead furrowed with the question.

"Got t' repo't Monday. New junior high school on Adamsville Road."

"Man, you'll like it. Real sharp!"

Bobbie stared at the brown shag rug on the yellowish, pine wood floor. His face drawn taut with a serious expression; Bobbie whispered as if he were speaking only to himself, forcing Alvin to lean forward to hear the words, "Don't think I'm gonna be goin' fo' long." After a short pause, he said, "Seventeen an' still in junior high." He looked up at Alvin. "Think I'd be wastin' my time stayin' in school? Better off gettin' a job?"

Alvin wasn't ready for the questions. He didn't have the answers and could only hedge. "Better see Mr. Finn about quittin'."

"Wants me t' give it a try first. If'n I don't do good, might let me quit. Maybe I'm not gonna do good. Lot worser then befo'. Then maybe they'll let me quit. Think so?"

"That's one way," Alvin answered, then added: "another way is to get some teacher mad, or give all your teachers a bad time. The principal'll call up Mr. Finn and tell him to take your bad ass out, pronto!" They had a laugh over that one. But while Bobbie was laughing, he made the serious, final decision to quit school. How? He didn't care. He just wanted out.

Bobbie's get-out-of-school campaign worked. By the end of the first semester in January, his marks were either failures or very poor. He had managed to flunk English, history and general mathematics; D's in science and woodshop with an unsatisfactory in physical education. Bobbie beamed a wide smile, when he saw his report

163

card. He was satisfied. He voiced his feelings to no one in particular as he walked down the main corridor, "Now, maybe I'll get outta this goddam place!"

It wasn't long, before Mr. Finn was contacted by the school counselor, who in turn contacted Bobbie, who was waiting expectantly.

"Your marks were terrible, Bobbie! Mr. Harbert said . . . you don't have any interest in your school work. And your conduct isn't good. Give your teachers too much back talk. Don't cooperate with the counselor. I'd like to know, just what's the trouble!" Mr. Finn was upset. His neck was changing from pink to red like a boiling lobster. He was staring at Bobbie with controlled patience, waiting for the explanation.

Bobbie, never one to hurry, when he knew an angry adult was waiting, stalled for effect. He put on a serious, intent face and muttered, "Well . . . I guess . . . guess . . . I jes don't like school."

"You mean you want to quit school don't you?"

Bobbie waited a moment, then answered, "Yeah . . . guess that's it."

"That's about the only thing left to do, since school's a complete waste of time for you and the entire school staff!"

After an awkward silence, James Finn rose from the living room chair with his briefcase at his side and said, "I'll make the necessary arrangements to end your school career, Bobbie. We'll get you working papers. You'll soon find out that working isn't much fun. Youll miss the easy life you had in school. Report to school as usual tomorrow, and everyday after that until we complete the paperwork." He took four giant steps to the front door, said good-bye to the Hills and Bobbie and left.

Mrs. Hill looked at Mr. Hill, who eased the situation

by addressing Bobbie in his soft, drawling voice, "He's right Bobbie. . . . Workin' ain't no fun. . . . Have some money in your pockets. . . . Still ain't no fun."

Bobbie didn't answer. He kept staring at the floor and its oak strips, noticing they needed a resanding and a coat of shellac.

CHAPTER 23

Despite February's assortment of foul weather, rain, fog, snow and gusty winds, Bobbie left school officially, got working papers and suffered through four job interviews at the state's Employment Security Office. The employment officer labeled Bobbie as best suited for light manual labor only; nothing too strenuous, physical or mental, because of his small size and poor school record. After a lengthy screening of the job file, the employment officer finally placed Bobbie with the Hearthside Restaurant. It was a bus boy and kitchen helper job at forty-eight dollars a week with supper included.

"Ain't much, but it'll do fo' now," Bobbie said to himself, when he left the office to report to the restaurant to meet the owner, a Mr. Camerino.

The resaurant was located on a side street off Colony Road. It was a modern, white clapboard and red clay brick, one story affair with a rustic, field stone chimney. Bobbie had trouble finding the restaurant the first trip but after the first week, he became familiar with the new section of town. He liked working in the high-priced restaurant with its radiant decorations: the deep, wine-colored carpeting, green-tinted pine paneling decorated with original oil paintings, the charming white and pink marble fireplace with hand-carved oak mantel and the teakwood cocktail bar. Bobbie was satisfied with the job even though his salary was minimal. His employer was friendly, the work wasn't too hard, the other workers were helpful and he was finished by 10:00 p.m. five nights a week.

Bobbie hadn't seen Rayford in over a year, and wanted to take advantage of the job to see him again. During the first week, Bobbie became friendly with one of the colored chefs, who lived in East Mercerton and promised him a ride downtown. He wanted to stop by the luncheonette the first Saturday night he worked, figuring Rayford would be at the corner hangout with Shorty and Lenny.

It was 10:30 p.m., when Bobbie slammed the car door shut, thanked the chef and waved good-bye. He was dressed in his black winter pants with a heavy, woolen, red plaid shirt under his knee length, black overcoat. But he still shivered. The night air was frigid and the corner sidewalk in front of the luncheonette was empty. Its vapor clouded windows hid the inside with a gray, watery blur.

Bobbie stepped gingerly over a patch of ice on the bottom step. He opened the door quietly and walked over to the counter. With rapid, jerking eye movement, he stole a look at every face. Only strangers stared back at him. The long room didn't have a familiar face; not even the man behind the counter, who asked in an irritated voice, after waiting for Bobbie's attention, "Well, whatcha want?"

Bobbie glanced to either side of the counter stool and then at the short, pudgy stranger in the apron; opened his mouth as if to ask the question that was on his mind, hesitated, then changed his mind and ordered coffee. He sat on the hard-cushioned stool covered with worn red leather, sipping the hot liquid brew that was masquerading as coffee. He kept asking himself questions, but knowing he didn't have the answers. "Rayford still 'round? . . .

Maybe got caught muggin'? . . . Was turnin' eighteen, when I lef' . . . If'n he got caught . . . mus' be in jail!" Bobbie glanced around, feeling uneasy but glad no one could read his mind. "No use jumpin' 'head myself. Puttin' Rayford in jail, befo' I find out what happened," he thought, while laughing to himself.

He got the owner's attention again and leaned forward. "Say, do ya know a guy name, Rayford Elston? Use t' hang 'round here with two other guys, Shorty and Lenny. I'm tryin' t' get in touch with 'em."

The owner's irritated look changed to mild alarm as he tried to get his mind working. Bobbie sat patiently, while the owner rubbed his neck and stared at the coffee stained counter. After a lengthy two minutes rubbing his neck, the owner finally remembered. The mental victory brightened his swarthy complexion, making his black eyes shine. His long, thin lips parted noisily, and he spoke with effort. The words came out in a thick accent. Bobbie had to lean forward again and ask for a repeat, making a quick translation of the garbled speech. It turned out that Rayford and his partners were now in the state prison. They had gotten into trouble raping a girl, before the Christmas holidays.

Bobbie left the place, after finishing his coffee, angry at himself for not getting to Rayford sooner. He walked down the sidewalk looking for a cab, complaining to himself; "Shoulda come 'round soon's I got out. Waited too goddamn long! Man, I'm never gonna learn!"

Bobbie hailed an empty cab, its roof covered with snow from a recent storm. He got in, gave the Hill's address, sat back in the black leather seat and said to himself, "Might jes go on home. Ain't never gonna see Rayford 'gain!" He rode home in silence.

The work routine and his limited free time finally

killed whatever glamor and attraction the job held for
Bobbie. This changed his attitude from satisfaction to
extreme discontent in a little more than six months. By
August, Bobbie was so disgusted with the work, he
wanted to quit. But knew he couldn't.

It was Monday, August 13th and Bobbie had the day
off. He was lounging in tee shirt and shorts, since he was
alone. The radio was on but he wasn't listening to it.
"Ain't this somethin'. My birthday t'day an' can't even
buy myself a present," Bobbie said in a loud voice to the
empty room. He looked down at the two one-dollar bills
and four dimes lying in his palm. "Needs this fo' bus fare.
Can't even spen' it!"

Bobbie didn't tell anyone it was his eighteenth birthday. He didn't want any fuss; like a silly birthday cake
or presents. Bobbie would rather do without a present
than accept one from somebody in the foster home. He
didn't want to give them the impression he was begging
for a present. It wasn't that he disliked the Hills or his
foster brothers, he didn't feel like one of them. It was just
someplace to stay.

The afternoon dragged on slowly with the Hills out
shopping, and the other boys working at summer jobs.
Bobbie interrupted his discontented reverie to get up and
shut off the radio, then took off his damp, sticky tee shirt.
It was a hot, humid, August day. Back in the chair, he
propped his right leg over the chair's worn right arm and
let his thoughts have free play. "Rayford was sharp. . . .
Showed me how t' get money fas'—'stead I'm bustin' my
ass fo' peanuts. . . . Yeah. . . . peanuts. . . . Time I pays
board. . . . buys clothes. . . . ain't got nothin' lef' fo'
spendin' money. . . . Can't even save fo' a car. . . . If'n I
had me a sharp car. . . . get me some nice broads. . . .
Have me a ball!"

Without any improvement in Bobbie's attitude or situation, August dragged into September. He kept comparing his present, dull life against the exciting nights with Rayford and the easy money. It wasn't long, before Bobbie decided to try again for easy money. He felt good about it inside, and kept it to himself. It was exciting just to think about it. Bobbie's spirits perked up, because he enjoyed making plans. He spent most of his time thinking about it. It was fun going over each little detail.

Bobbie was going "underground" and he had that satisfied feeling; like the feeling you get when you come home from a long trip. He was going back. But this time it would be different. He told himself, "Gonna work alone . . . Got caught befo'. . . . Woulda got caught with Rayford. . . . Better off workin' alone. . . . Nobody t' goof me up."

With his plans settled, Bobbie worked on getting a pistol. He was going all-out this time. Getting a gun was easy. Within two weeks, he bought a thirty-eight caliber pistol, plus an ample supply of bullets. It took all of Bobbie's meager savings, plus that week's spending money— but he was in business. His kind of business.

Bobbie rubbed the barrel and fondled the stock, smiling contentedly, before he hid it in the bottom of his suitcase, making a secret compartment for it and the lead bullets; a deadly, private arsenal. Bobbie put the suitcase in the back of the closet and closed the door, then whispered to himself, "I'm ready. . . . Gonna be a big one, too!" He stuck his head out first, looked down the hall and listened. It was empty and silent. Satisfied, he walked down the stairs and joined the others at the supper table for a quiet Sunday supper.

That night in bed, Bobbie thought about his present situation and his past mistakes. He thought about the one big mistake, trying to take too many bulky articles from the gas station that vague night, so long ago. How many years was it? He tried to remember. Deciding it was at least four, he went back to his thoughts. "We could pull muggin' jobs an' get 'way in the car . . . Me alone, man. . . . can't do nothin' like that an' get 'way with it!" He continued his rambling, "Needs t' hit a place with small stuff. Stick it in my pockets, with nobody noticin'." After a long pause, his puzzled face brightened. He said out loud, "Like watches an' wallets. . . jewel'ry, too!"

He stared into the darkness for a long time—thinking. Before he went to sleep that night, he made up his mind. It would be a jewelry store. Which one? He didn't know, that was the next problem. But he would enjoy solving it.

Bobbie became more remote as his temporary plans became final ones and he collected his tools. It was almost as if he were afraid someone would read his thoughts. His withdrawn attitude was noticed by everyone in the foster home and it puzzled them. Mrs. Hill mentioned it to her husband, who suggested they talk to Alvin first, before talking to Bobbie.

Mr. Hill was standing by the doorway leading to the dining room, watching for Bobbie, while Mrs. Hill questioned Alvin.

"Bobbie been talkin' to you, Alvin?" Mrs. Hill asked. Her black-skinned, round, broad-featured face looked flatter and broader. Her dark eyes squinted with the question.

"No, Mam, ain't been doin' no talkin' to me. Ain't been doin' no talkin' to nobody," Alvin said. His long, angular face, dark skin and black eyes blended into a convincing blank expression.

Mrs. Hill wasn't satisfied with the answer and probed again, "Sure he don't say nothin'. Not even in his sleep."

She learned forward and squinted again. A jelly-like ripple rolled around her wide middle, like it was on the merry-go-round.

"How do I know he talks in his sleep? Jus' lays on his back, starin' up at the ceilin'. I'm not waitin' for him to talk in his sleep. I'm sleepin' way before him."

"Jus stares at the ceiling, Alvin?" Mr. Hill asked. A puzzled look spread over his brown, big-featured face. He stared at Alvin with small black eyes set far apart on his wide face.

"Jus lays there. Don't talk at all!" Alvin exclaimed in a loud voice, and was waved down by Mr. Hill. He continued, "Used to be good talkin' buddies at night. You know, tell each other everythin'."

"Maybe we ought to tell his caseworker. . . . Parole officer, too. See what they say, before we talks to Bobbie," Mr. Hill suggested, rubbing the back of his long, thick neck with his long, heavy fingers.

"I'll call Mr. Finn tomorrow. Explain about Bobbie," Mrs. Hill decided.

When Mrs. Hill called, Mr. Finn couldn't give any attention to Bobbie's case. He had been given an emergency placement assignment for a family group of five children. He was in the middle of making final arrangements for their placement into foster homes, and was forced to let Bobbie's case wait until he got the five children settled in homes.

Mr. Finn's delay allowed enough time for Bobbie to make five trips into the business district. He looked over every jewelry store; its size, location, back alley, rear entrance, windows and doors. He noticed one store in particular. It had a rear entrance from the alleyway with bars protecting the doorway and windows at ground level, but had an unbarred lavatory window that was too small for the average adult to even think of crawling through. Bobbie checked this window carefully. He decided he could get his small, narrow body through it. Bobbie made up his mind, standing in the alley, looking up at the window. This was it. He was going through that window. All he would need would be a small ladder or a pile of boxes. The rest would be as easy as spreading butter on a hot roll.

Bobbie decided the next day, which was Friday, to make the "hit" that Saturday night after work. He figured the police would be busy with drunks and barroom fights. They wouldn't be as free as on weekday nights. "Yeah, this Saturday is it!" Bobbie said, almost too loud, while he was dressing for work that Friday afternoon. He was in a confident mood, feeling good about the whole thing. "I'll start talkin' 'gain," he decided, when he went downstairs to say good-bye to Mrs. Hill, who noticed the change, becoming doubly confused.

CHAPTER 24

When Harry Rivers graduated from high school, he knew college was out of the question. Because of family obligations, he had to take his first full-time job at age eighteen. But it was during this early part of his working career that he became interested in law enforcement. Harry studied everything he could get his eager hands on about the subject. Even as a boy, he had admired policemen in their blue uniforms and got his biggest thrill, when a police officer let him touch his shiny black holster and pistol. He never forgot the feel of the stiff leather holster and the cold steel pistol.

It wasn't until six years after high school, that Harry finally made it. The police academy graduation had been held on a typically hot, humid, July day but he didn't mind the heat. Harry was too happy to think about it. It may have been a second choice, considering that college was his first choice, but it was more real to him. And this was all that mattered, now.

Harry's achievement was more than just personal success. He was one of a first group of Negroes appointed to Mercerton's police force. It was a major breakthrough for his race. Mercerton's policemen had always been white. Harry and the other Negroes realized what it meant and were anxious to make good and justify their appointments.

Harry's first real ambition was to play football for a major college but it had to die a quick death, even though his high school grades averaged a B+, while majoring in the academic course. His college board test scores were high enough, and he had graduated in the upper quarter of his class. Harry had been a two-year letterman; playing fullback on the high school team and was offered football scholarships by two, Big Ten, midwestern schools. He had to reject both scholarship offers, when his father was stricken by a heart attack. The hospital expenses and the family's support fell on his youthful but muscular shoulders. He was forced to take a dull job driving a freight delivery truck for the Seashore Railroad Company. The routine was boring but he got use to it and let his strong body enjoy the heavy work hauling freight.

Job followed job in a monotonous series; from the dull, truck driving job to construction laborer and finally to a deathly life in an automobile parts factory. Harry hated factory work with a passion. It not only killed his natural senses, dulling his keen mind, but the monotony of the assembly line drained the spring out of his muscles. It made him lazy. Harry wanted out, before he became stagnant.

The best thing that ever happened to Harry Rivers was meeting pretty, pleasant, Caroline Price. She was the one who lured him out of his doldrums, getting him to become active at the Negro Community House, and introducing him into her socially active world. Caroline not only attracted others with her good looks but her friendly way of putting people at ease and a willingness to understand and accept others was the charm that made one a friend for life. It was a relaxing pleasure to be in her company.

Through Caroline's influence, Harry became a volunteer instructor in the physical training department for the Negro Community House on Wilson Street and also became active in the local organization for better race relations and a better life for Negroes. He enjoyed working with the boys at the community house and was a favorite with them. They were in constant competition, trying to outdo each other in being helpful. A boy felt great, when Harry let him carry the basketball, a jacket or just to have Harry's friendly arm around his shoulder.

All during this period, Harry continued to study law enforcement, juvenile delinquency and any related subject. When the opportunity came, he applied for the city's police officer position. Harry passed the open competitive test, placing at the eight position of the first ten out of a total group of seventy-five candidates.

The day he got his official acceptance notice, instructing him to report for training at the city's police academy, Harry's eyes became moist, his throat thumpy and his voice hoarse. He wasn't embarrassed; they were tears of happiness. He let his wife kiss them away. Then she began her own brand of free flowing tears—female style. The baby joined them, making it a tearful threesome.

The rigorous physical training, combined with the academic work, challenged Harry's total ability. He took to it like an addicted gambler takes to the dice tables in Las Vegas. Harry loved the firearms training; the feel of the thirty-eight caliber, firm and cold in his grip and its powerful, bucking surge that pulled his arm upward and to the right. He absorbed its strength and power, gaining confidence in his growing handling skill.

It was a new, intriguing world of weapons and Harry soon discovered he had a talent for pistol firing on the range. He became a good shot and was nicknamed, Hot Shot Harry, by the other trainees.

He even enjoyed the long hours studying the dry, dull, law books, rules, regulations and policeman's manuals on firearms and protocol. The harder the work, the harder he worked. Harry had to make it—and he did.

Standing as tall and erect as he could in his blue uniform, Harry followed the line down the aisle. They were getting their diplomas; the piece of paper that said you had sweated through eight long weeks of tough, rigid training—eight weeks of plain, hard work. He almost floated up the steps to the podium and shook hands with the mayor, receiving his "union card" into the select group. It was the final act breathing new life into his self-image.

Harry began his active career at the bottom, walking the sidewalks. His area was Mercerton's main business district, with its many theaters, stores, shops and restaurants. He liked the busy streets; the people in a hurry and the slow moving traffic. It made him feel alive, a part of something. But it did have a drawback. There were too many stores with rear alley entrances, compelling Harry to keep a close check on them.

The warm summer weather gave way to October's cool breezes. Those beautiful days of warm sunshine, yet not hot, cool breezes, yet not cold; the crystal clear, pleasant days of autumn.

Harry always got up early during autumn. He loved the just right weather, and that particular Saturday was no exception. Being a "health bug," he did push-ups and knee bends in the small bedroom, between the baby's crib and the bed. He never failed to bump into the bed and the crib, waking the baby and Caroline, the heavy sleeper, looked at Harry with half-closed, bleary eyes as if he were crazy. The baby, Darleen, didn't like the rude, bedroom gymnastics. She cried big tears, swinging her arms and kicking the crib, upsetting the morning's peaceful air.

Having succeeded in getting everyone up early that morning, Harry made up for it by cooking a big breakfast: hot oatmeal, bacon, and eggs, toast and coffee. The bacon and coffee odors blended into one and filled the small

177

apartment pleasantly but completely. Caroline was quiet and slow moving, but managed to eat in spite of her foggy morning vision and slow reflexes.

Harry ate quietly, laughing silently at his sleepy wife with her heavy, drooping eyelids and his noisy daughter. He sipped his coffee, making a loud, slurping noise. It always got her attention. She hated coffee slurping. "Honey, I was thinking, why don't we look at those houses?" Harry asked, not letting her attention wander back to her food.

She raised her head. Opened her right eye a little more than her left for a clear view and said in her usual, hoarse, early morning voice, "Is that why you got me up so early?" Her heart-shaped face was attractive, even in the morning. It was delicately featured with everything evenly matched; small nose, fine lips and pointed chin. Her skin was light brown and soft and she had black eyes with a friendly gleam, alert to life, once she became fully awake. Her hair was black and long with a natural curl.

"Guess you might say that," Harry confessed with a grin. "Getting tired of three small rooms." His grin changed to a serious frown, then he said, "Bet the bears at the zoo have more living space!"

"Can't argue with you there, honey, I'm tired of bumping into furniture, too!" Caroline replied, with a more agreeable tone in her voice. The coffee was lifting her early morning drowsiness, like the sun burning off the fog at the seashore. She continued, "The two off Old Lane Avenue? What street was it?"

"I think. . . Wait, I'll get the paper." Harry flipped the pages of last night's paper, until he came to the real estate ads. "Here they are. . . They're both on DeWitt Avenue. Nice neighborhood near the high school. Going colored. Won't have any trouble getting in. . . I guess. . .

If we got enough for a down payment." Harry lifted his face above the paper and looked at Caroline. His face was all angles with wide cheekbones, pointed chin and a wide, ski jump nose. He had a clear, brown-skinned complexion with faint scar tissue over his brows; a left over from his football days.

"Don't have much of that," Caroline said.

"Don't forget, I've got a steady position now. Means a lot when you apply for a mortgage," Harry replied. "Let's hustle out and take a look."

They toured both houses; one in the morning and the other during the early afternoon. Caroline loved the single, white clapboard, two story with the red brick fireplace and paneled basement. Harry had liked it too. They decided to see about getting enough money for the down payment but agreed to wait until the following Monday, realizing that Saturday the banks and loan offices were closed.

Caroline was excited, never expecting to see a house she liked and wanted on their first house hunting trip. It had been an enjoyable day. Even the baby had been good. Caroline chirped all the way up the stairs to their third floor apartment; "Oh, Harry! Can't stop thinking about that beautiful fireplace. That lovely knotty pine in the basement. Think of all the nice parties we can have. Can't wait to tell the gang."

"Now wait a minute, honey. Haven't put a down payment on the house, yet. Don't get too excited. Wait until we get approved for a mortgage," Harry said, trying to keep calm about the house. But his plea for restraint wasn't convincing. Caroline kept up a steady stream of chatter about the house during the rest of the afternoon, while Harry dressed for work.

Fully dressed in his uniform, Harry stood in the archway between the kitchen and bedroom, his six-foot, two-inch, 225 pound, muscular frame filled the archway. He asked, "Well, how do I look?"

"Like a cop," Caroline teased, stopped feeding the baby and gave Harry a long look. She took in the neat fit of the blue jacket, the muscular chest and wide shoulders filling it completely. She admired the sharply creased, blue trousers, the black, highly polished, leather holster, cartridge belt and strap with shiny, gray, thirty-eight caliber bullets; the clean, gleaming black pistol resting in its holster, the silver badge on his blue jacket and silver police emblem on his blue hat. "He's a handsome man, this cop-husband of mine," Caroline thought. She ran over to kiss him good-bye.

"Say, honey, that was some kiss!" Harry said, out of breath, when they parted from the embrace. "You know I got to go to work," he said in a breathy voice.

"Yes, isn't that a shame." Caroline's long, feminine fingers caressed his chest. She gazed up into his face with half-closed eyes. "Come home early, honey."

They both laughed, kissed again and then walked together with their arms around each other over to the baby. She had watched the love scene with infant indifference. Harry tickled Darleen under her chubby, moon-shaped face and kissed her on the left cheek. She giggled a big smile and waved her arms at her father. Harry gave her another kiss on the right cheek for good measure and she waved her arms and laughed at him again. Harry and Caroline walked out of the kitchen into the hallway and kissed good-bye again. He promised to get home as early as possible. Caroline watched him walk down the stairs, with a happy feeling inside. He was her man.

CHAPTER 25

Saturday night for Bobbie Lee meant work until ten, clearing dirty dishes from the cluttered tables and helping the chefs clean and close the kitchen. Bobbie hated his work even more that night. Without talking to any of the chefs, he followed their directions mutely. He worked from habit, leaving himself free to think about . . . later. Bobbie mulled over each detail, smugly satisfied with himself. No one suspected. He felt secure and with a little luck, he'd get in and out of the store without getting caught.

Harry Rivers contentedly walked his "beat" that night. He stopped at each store, trying the door and sending a yellow triangle through the long, dark interior. He was enjoying the crispy cool night air. The wool uniform didn't feel heavy or warm. He walked along sidewalks crowded with slow moving strollers getting in the way of those hurrying to catch the second show at the downtown movies. Everyone seemed to be enjoying the night breeze. It glided by in cool, windy gusts and swirls, sending dry brown leaves and scraps of paper scurrying on to nowhere.

Bobbie sat quietly on the bus, heading for Slate and Enterprise; the intersection of the city's two main streets and the center of the business district. He reached inside his shirt and felt the pistol. It was like holding a piece of ice; hard and cold. He played with the extra bullets in his jacket's right pocket, letting them slip through his fingers. Bobbie checked the safety catch on the pistol again, making sure it was in the safe position. He wanted to avoid an accident. It wasn't necessary to check the regular-size flashlight, the small flashlight or the screwdriver. They felt bulky and pressed against his body, pulling his jacket collar down against his neck. He said to himself, while looking at the other passengers: "Don't know from nothin'. None of 'em. Gonna walk off nice an' quiet. Nobody'll see nothin'. Man . . . gonna be a good night!"

Harry's early hours were quiet but pleasant. He had been reporting by telephone at the various corner check points in his area, and the last checkpoint had been at the corner of East Slate and Lambert at 10:00 p.m. He had telephoned in a routine report that everything was quiet. Harry was taking his time, feeling in no hurry as he walked down East Slate Street. He said to himself, loud enough to be heard, when he tried the lock on Levin's Jewelry Store and beamed his flashlight through the glass front;"Better check the alley doors on my way back."

Bobbie stepped carefully off the bus at Slate and Enterprise, not caring to jar anything loose or make a lot of noise. He kept both hands in his jacket pockets, separating his tools. On the sidewalk Bobbie looked around slowly, then crossed Slate Street and followed Enterprise to Hanford. He crossed Enterprise and hurried down Hanford Street, glad to see it deserted. Bobbie relaxed and slowed his pace, walking at a regular stride. He stopped at Cliff Street, glanced both directions, then crossed it briskly. Hopping onto the sidewalk, Bobbie continued down Hanford Street, becoming more confident as he neared his destination; circling in as if he were a lion, getting in position to spring on a grazing antelope.

At Hanford and Lambert, Bobbie paused for a moment. Some of his confidence suddenly floated away, leaving an empty feeling in his stomach. It was a funny kind of sensation. He began sweating in spite of the cool air, when he turned right and headed down Lambert Street. At the alley's entrance, parallel to East Slate and Hanford, Bobbie got that funny feeling again. His palms were sweaty inside his pockets. His forehead and armpits were damp, and his stomach made gaseous, gurgling sounds. He tried to look around casually, failed in his attempt and stepped awkwardly into the alley's darkness. Bobbie stopped at the first doorway to count the buildings and set his position. The pause helped a little. His pulse and heartbeat slowed down to a normal rate. He felt better; not so nervous.

Bobbie located the store's rear section. It was the sixth one from the corner. He made a last check of the empty, silent alley, then walked quickly but quietly to the rear of Levin's Jewelry store. He placed two garbage-filled crates under the lavatory window. After digging easily into the decayed window sill, Bobbie worked the long screwdriver through the wood and released the inside latch, then pushed the window up and out of the way. A minute later, he was inside.

Harry turned right at East Slate and Cliff, walked slowly up Cliff and paused at the alley's entrance. He looked down the narrow, dark corridor and hesitated, peering through the ink black darkness. Harry couldn't see a thing. He had to go into the alley. "Better check," he said to himself. Harry stepped quietly into the alley, listening to every step, trying to remain calm and alert. The quiet, dark alley made him feel uneasy. His grating footsteps added to the tense feeling. It lay over him like a thick, morning mist. Harry couldn't get rid of the nervous feeling, and it became worse as he walked further into the eerie darkness.

It was dark inside the jewelry store. But Bobbie managed to navigate from the rear storeroom to the long, rectangular-shaped salesroom in the front of the building

183

without an accident. Once in the front salesroom, he was able to see fairly well, without risking his flashlight. The street light beamed in a pale, yellowish light. It was enough for his work. He took all the change and bills from the open cash register drawer. He reached inside a display counter and lifted twenty watches from their carrying cases and put them around his wrists, working his way up his thin arms. The diamond rings, pins and assorted jewelry, which he didn't waste valuable time to identify, were quickly stuffed into his empty trouser pockets. When he finished, Bobbie waited, listening to the silence. He remained upright and still for a final check, before moving out of the salesroom towards the rear of the building. "Got me a nice haul. Easy too!" Bobbie said to himself as he walked one careful step at a time, out of the salesroom. He didn't want to upset anything. "Doin' real good! Don't goof now!" Bobbie coached himself, while feeling his way around the last display counter, before treading through the dark storeroom. He beamed his flashlight and cut a yellow path through the darkness, then shut it off when he came to the lavatory door.

Harry was next to Levin's Jewelry Store. He had just tried the rear door and inspected the rear windows of the neighboring music shop, when he heard strange sounds, as if someone were struggling out of a window. Harry froze in the doorway. He inched his right hand down to unsnap the holster. After he drew out the revolver, he cupped his hands over the trigger area and released the safety catch, muffling the sharp, snapping click. Harry stayed inside the doorway. From his concealed position, he watched the dark, shadowy form, not more than twenty-five feet away, struggle through the small window opening.

Bobbie stuck his arms straight out and used the crates for support, gradually working the lower half of his body through the window that was hardly big enough for his narrow frame. After he reached the ground and before he could collect himself, Bobbie was stunned by a loud, excited voice. "Don't move! Put your hands up!" Before the last word had echoed off the nearby brick wall, Bobbie started running down the alley—away from the voice.

Harry sprung into action, chasing the fleeting shadow and shouted his final order, "Stop or I'll shoot!"

The command was ignored.

Harry's brain became a whirling computer, issuing commands to his right hand holding the pistol. Shoot! Shoot! His arm felt numb, while his trigger finger squeezed twice. Two sharp blasts erupted from the barrel. He felt the sudden, bucking recoil.

The last shouting command, the two loud shots and the screaming ricochets off the brick wall startled Bobbie. He stopped running, crouched against the brick wall and reached inside his jacket. Taking out the shiny pistol, Bobbie extended both arms. He held the pistol with both hands and took aim at the dark, running figure. It was getting closer; an easier, larger target. He fired twice.

Harry saw the small, crouched shadow and the shiny glint off the short, narrow barrel. He heard the first shot, felt the second. His trigger finger fired twice at the small human target crouched against the brick wall, after he heard the first shot and saw its flashing red flame in the alley's darkness.

The high street light on the Lambert Street side of the alley beamed feeble, yellow rays. One could hardly see the two small streams trickling down the alley's incline, blending their red pureness with its dirt. In the center, they met and collected into a common pool. Then, they began their joint venture toward the sewer drain, at the end of the alley.